LIVING WITHOUT JUSTICE

LIVING WITHOUT JUSTICE

Loren R. Fisher

WIPF & STOCK · Eugene, Oregon

LIVING WITHOUT JUSTICE

Wipf & Stock
An Imprint of Wipf and Stock Publishers
199 W. 8th Ave., Suite 3
Eugene, OR 97401
www.wipfandstock.com

ISBN 13: 978-1-61097-302-1

Cataloguing-in-Publication data:

Fisher, Loren R.
      Living without justice / Loren R. Fisher.

      x + 174 p. ; 23cm.

      ISBN 13: 978-1-61097-302-1

      1. Bible. O.T.—Fiction. 2. Job (Biblical figure). I. Title.

PS3606 F57 2013

Manufactured in the USA

For Susan
1953–2010

Vanishing Flakes
Early this morning there was snow on the deck.
It arrived quietly in large white flakes.
By 11:00 am the snow was gone,
The sun was out, and the steam was rising.

The flakes came down, but the moisture returned.
It was all so fast, and it did not last.
The picture is clear. Our moments create:
Brush strokes in a large landscape! Beautiful!

So, I shout, "Violence," and I am not answered;
I cry for help, and there is no justice.

JOB 19:7

Acknowledgments

I AM INDEBTED TO my teachers, my colleagues, and to my students. My teachers taught me to work with ancient texts and to use multiple tools for deciphering and understanding them. My colleagues helped me to evaluate my findings. Working in this way I experienced many changes in my thinking along an exciting and adventurous road. My students reminded me that they loved their freedom. They were all different. Their strengths and interests were varied, and they resisted any attempt to mold them into a school of thought. They inspired me to follow them.

Stefan Heym's novel, *The King David Report* (1973), fascinated my students, my family, and me. This novel earned a place in the bibliography for my class on The History of Israel. Many times, my students commented on the importance of this novel and suggested that we needed a few more. I thought about their suggestions and decided to write a novel about scribal life in the time of King David. *Living without Justice* is the third historical novel in my trilogy about the scribes of Israel. In the first novel, *The Jerusalem Academy,* I wrote an Afterword, which discusses the importance of historical novels for historical studies. When history is only the stage for a novel, that novel is not a historical novel. An authentic historical novel uses real people and fictional people; both are necessary. Also the places are real, and the events are actual occasions. In addition, fictional elements are essential in narrating the response of the people as they experience these events.

My wife, Jane, is an excellent writer and editor. She helps me not only with my manuscripts, but she listens to my discussions of my work that unduly dominate our table talk.

Acknowledgments

I want to thank K. C. Hanson, my editor at Wipf and Stock Publishers, whose keen insight springs from the fact that he is also a proven scholar of Ancient Mediterranean Literature.

Loren R. Fisher
Medford, Oregon
7 December 2011

Abbreviations

BCE	Before the Common Era
CE	The Common Era
1 & 2 Chr	1 & 2 Chronicles
Deut	Deuteronomy
EA	El Amarna
Exod	Exodus
Gen	Genesis
Isa	Isaiah
Judg	Judges
1 & 2 Kgs	1 & 2 Kings
l.p.h.	life, prosperity, health
p	page
pp	pages
1 & 2 Sam	1 & 2 Samuel

Prologue

MY NAME IS NAAM. I am the son of Jonathan and Keziah. In the following text, I will narrate my story and my family's activities during the last part of David's reign in Jerusalem and during Solomon's reign. My mother wrote the first two books in this series. In her first book, *The Jerusalem Academy*, she writes about how *The Royal Epic* (*Genesis*) was compiled by my father and his fellow scribes at The Jerusalem Academy. In her second book, *The Minority Report,* she focused on my father's poem, *The Rebel Job*. In this third book, I will continue our story and include our friends who lived and worked at The Jerusalem Academy. Also, I will relate experiences from my life that illustrate the central point in *The Rebel Job*: there is no justice.

At the age of twenty I became a teacher in the academy where I was able to continue the work and interests of my father and mother, plus my own special interest in all things Egyptian. Also, I was fortunate to have the help of a small group of teachers and friends who were not bound by old traditions. Old traditions are important, but they must be sifted. At The Jerusalem Academy we rejected some traditions while we rescued others. All of this was done in the context of the international scene and with the aim of moving toward a new future. We had the desire and ability to extend our horizons, but after the death of King David, his heir, King Solomon, instituted policies that enslaved our people and proved once again that there is no justice.

1

THE DAY I MET Khety—a scribe and teacher from Egypt—is a day that I will always remember. As I look back, I realize my life changed course that day. I was about fourteen at the time. Khety was in Jerusalem interviewing for a teaching position in the academy. My father brought him to our home for dinner, and I remember asking him what Egyptians would serve at such a dinner. He gave us a typical menu using the Egyptian words and showed us how these words were written. From that moment my mother and I became interested in the Egyptian language. Meeting Khety was only one of the great moments I experienced growing up in Jerusalem, but it was a pivotal moment. I fell in love with the Egyptian language and culture, and this has placed its mark on my teaching and writing at The Jerusalem Academy. This is what makes the academy such an interesting place: there are teachers and students from many other cities, and there is always an air of excitement surrounding new discoveries, foreign news, or new translations of foreign literature.

My father has mentioned on several occasions that he learned a great deal about foreign countries from some of our teachers, but he also said that some of his most interesting information came from people who were working in Jerusalem. When David's palace was being constructed, he used many workmen from Tyre. Father talked with them about Tyre, about the ships that came to Tyre, and about the Egyptians and others who were just passing through. He also talked with David's mercenary guards, the Cherethites and Pelethites, who were from Crete and other islands in the far west, as were the Philistines. He noted, however, that many of the guards knew nothing about Crete or the islands, because their grandparents had arrived in this country with the invasions of the Sea Peoples about two hundred years ago. Some of them were born and raised at Beth-shan where the Sea Peoples had been mercenaries for many years, going back to the time of the Egyptian rule at Beth-shan. The ones from Beth-shan did know something about Crete, because their ancestors had kept alive some of their traditions. It is clear that these people have made some contributions to our own language, that is, the language of Canaan. One example is our use of their word *seren*, meaning, "lord" or "ruler." But my father says that the most important thing he has learned from all of these contacts is that all of us in our world—from Babylon to Crete and from Ugarit to Egypt—have a common cultural background. At times, even during periods when we are enemies, we all seem to remember, to write, to tell stories, to celebrate, and to worship in ways that reveal this common background. This common background does not mean that individual countries cannot make important and new contributions, but new contributions always have a world of old traditions to overcome—both foreign and local.

The location of the academy in Jerusalem is also important. Other academies in places like Tyre or ancient Ugarit probably receive information as to recent events before we do, but our weather, especially in the summer, is so much better for our work. The inhabitants of coastal cities have to endure hot and muggy days in the summer while at the same time our thin air is invigorating. True, they have the sea to extend their horizons, but we have the exciting views from the mountains. When looking east from the Judean mountains and down toward the Salt Sea, I have often marveled at how the layers of dirt and rock have been twisted and turned in past ages. This landscape is so different from the horizontal layers of earth that make up the lowlands to the west or can be seen in the Egyptian hieroglyph for earth (Egyptian *ta'* represented by a horizontal bar). The sea seems so constant, but the mountains cause one to think about the changes that have occurred in the story of our earth. Living in Jerusalem has made me aware that not only do people change, but the earth changes as well.

So the academy and Jerusalem are important to me; I love them dearly. This is not to say that things are perfect here. In the city we have to be aware of the presence King David and his administration, even his prophets and priests. Especially the priests are difficult, and I must say that some teachers and students in the academy are conservative and always against any change or new thought. Such members of our community do not learn anything from our contacts with others or our mountains. They live in fear of King David, his priests, and his God, and their lives are dull and unrewarding. Among the minority, who are aware of our international setting and the opportunity we have to contribute something new to our world, there is a spirit of adventure, and that makes for an interesting and meaningful life.

2

MY MOTHER AND FATHER, Keziah and Jonathan, are wonderful parents and thoughtful members of the scribal community. They have lived at the Jerusalem Academy since its beginning just after David conquered Jerusalem. My father's most important works are: *The Royal Epic* (*Genesis*), which he edited with the help of others, and his poem, *The Rebel Job* (*Job* 3–26). My mother is also a writer. She has always kept a journal, and she has written *The Jerusalem Academy*, a book about our early years at the academy, and *The Minority Report*, a book that describes father's work on *The Rebel Job*. Both of her books show how our minds and our lives were shaped during those years.

During the first years of the Jerusalem Academy, we celebrated my grandfather Gad's seventieth birthday party. At the party, my parents also held a naming ceremony for their infant son in which mother read her poem:

> "Naam," we call forth his name.
> He will give us pleasant days;
> He will fill them with great songs.
> Goodness was ours when he came.
>
> We gave him a hero's name.
> Lives touched by him will be changed.
> He will sing of great events;
> We will never be the same.

My mother had high hopes for me. In her poem she drew upon every possible meaning of the word *na'am*. Though I try to be pleasant and good and can sing, as a mature adult I can assure you that I will probably never be a hero.

It was exciting growing up at The Jerusalem Academy, and my childhood was shaped by intellectuals who were drawn to the school. My family had many interesting friends, and they were all involved in projects that could very well change the direction of our lives and our state. My parents invited people into our home who brought growth, change, and happiness to all who were involved in their adventures. This was the case when my father, along with Elimelech and Elishama, produced the *Royal Epic*. They worked a long time searching for stories about the beginning of our world, and they gathered songs and stories about our fathers Abraham, Isaac, and Jacob. These stories and songs were commonly used in tomb rituals, and it was not an easy task to select the most appropriate stories and songs. They compiled the epic in order to bring unity to the separate states: Israel and Judah. In an epic all the people have to hear the stories and claim them as their stories.

My father, Elimelech, and Elishama were able to complete this epic in time for the dedication of David's palace. The dedication was a traditional seven-day celebration, and during that time our minstrels performed the entire epic. The people enjoyed this celebration, and it did help to unify them.

Some of the accomplishments of the academy were accompanied by problems and in some cases by dangers. Since the established leaders of both altar and state usually dislike new ideas that are essential to adventure, growth, and happiness, David and the priests did their best to hide my father's poem, *The Rebel Job*. Both altar and state went along with *The Ancient Story of Job*, which stressed the fear of God and obedience as the necessary prerequisites for a good, healthy, and long life. The ancient Job was patient and willing to bow before the creator in repentance for his sins (known or unknown). Thus, he received his reward. But this story was and still is a false illusion. Though threatened by certain priests, father maintained a contrasting opinion: the rebel Job was in touch with the real world and his views were important. The rebel said that the God of the orthodox was not all-powerful and that there was no justice (note God's hidden testing of the ancient Job). We all suffer in this world regardless of our situation. Father's Job wanted to build a meaningful life by helping others and blaming no one for life's difficulties. *The Rebel Job*, as I have said, is one example of our problems in the academy; it is a powerful example. It is a clear and critical word directed at the idea of retribution by an all-powerful God, and this idea was woven into the fabric of all our traditions: our chronicles, our stories, our laws, our psalms, and even the words of our prophets. But the priests believed that *The Rebel Job* would create a non-conforming public, and that the public would become impossible to rule. Mother's book, *The Minority Report*, deals with this issue in detail, but this is only one example of the kind of tension that existed between some of the scribes at the academy and those entrenched in positions of power in both altar and state. The tensions got better a little later, because Sheva, who was the head of the academy, reversed his rather blind support of altar and state. Also his wife, Sarah, and their daughter, Naomi, helped to convince Sheva to stand with his friends in the academy.

I do not want to give the impression that our life at the academy was always a life of producing great epics or of political tension. We had great times at weddings, parties, celebrations, and at home we always enjoyed our meals around the family table. As children we had great times at school, at play, and in the evenings we would go up on the roof of our house to tell stories. All our friends in The Jerusalem Academy, both adults and children, thought I would become a teacher in the academy. Also they were certain that Rachel, daughter of Elishama and Deborah, and I would be married one day. We grew up together; we went to school together; we helped to care for the other children. Rachel was beautiful and talented, and we sometimes talked about our future life together.

When I was twenty years old, I began to notice just how beautiful Rachel had become, and I was interested in becoming more than Rachel's good friend. Rachel seemed to be thinking along the same lines. When we were out walking one evening, I stopped and started to kiss her, but Rachel said, "No." She continued, "Naam, I have to tell you something. I'm in love with Samuel."

Samuel was a student from the academy, who had gone to Tyre to study with Zadok, a former teacher at The Jerusalem Academy. Samuel had returned recently to Jerusalem to continue his Babylonian studies with Magon, who was a great teacher and came to us from Tyre. I knew that Samuel was a fine student and a wonderful human being, but I was shocked, hurt, and speechless. I was not just angry with Rachel and Samuel; I was angry at everything and everyone. I kicked a large stone in the path and hurt my foot. As we walked back to the academy in total silence, I was limping, and I knew that Rachel was crying softly. I was devastated; I was disappointed and confused.

The next day I talked with mother about all of this. She was always helpful in difficult situations. She reminded me of what I had experienced in Beth-shan a few years earlier. "You told me that you enjoyed meeting Sharmila in Beth-shan," she said. "You said you felt guilty because you had always been so close to Rachel. But then you said that perhaps you and Rachel were more like a brother and a sister. I wonder. Does Rachel feel the same way?"

"That is possible. I do remember feeling guilty, and I was certainly attracted to Sharmila. She was beautiful, but there was more to it than that. When she came close to serve me some melon, I couldn't speak until a moment later. That event was not planned."

"Well, I doubt if Rachel planned 'her event.'"

"I suppose not. Also I remember when Sharmila came to Jerusalem with her father after our trip to Beth-shan, I had some of the same feelings for her. Even though we wrote a few letters after that, the distance did not allow our friendship to grow. Perhaps I should go up to Beth-shan; I would like to see Sharmila."

"You should wait a few weeks and see how you feel. Also you should write to her. It is possible, you should know, that she has found a 'Samuel.' In any case you need to have a clear head on your shoulders."

Mother was usually right. It took me several weeks to understand my feelings about all this. I did not talk with Rachel for some time, but I saw Samuel and her at the academy. Rachel did talk with mother and told her that she was sorry about all that had happened. But she said, "I could not help myself; it just happened." Then she added, "I will always love Naam; he is my brother."

"You should tell that to Naam," mother suggested.

That same day Rachel approached me. She took my hands in hers and said, "I will always stand by you. We have had a long history together. You will always be my brother."

"Thanks, and you tell Samuel that he is a lucky fellow."

"You can tell him. Let's go see him."

"Good idea."

We found Samuel, just leaving Magon's office. I said to him, "As you know Rachel and I are like brother and sister, and I want to tell you that you are one lucky fellow. Take good care of her."

I did write to Sharmila and received a great letter from her in return. She wrote that she would like to see me, and this would be possible, because her father, Abdi-anati, wanted to talk with my father and also with Khety and Magon. She would be coming with her father to Jerusalem in about two weeks. When I read this, I let out a shout for joy. Obviously, Sharmila had not met a "Samuel." In the letter she said that her father was still the only scribe at Beth-shan. She added, "During the last few years, I have been helping father with his work. I am grateful that father has taught me to read and write, and I like helping him. But there is still too much to do. We will be looking for a scribe who would like to come to Beth-shan."

There was a part of me that wanted to go to Beth-shan, but that was impossible. I was scheduled to teach some classes here in the academy in about two months. I thought, "If Sharmila and I were to marry, her father might need two scribes." These were wild thoughts. I would have to wait until Sharmila arrived. I did not know what would happen. But this I knew: it was going to be difficult to wait for two weeks.

I decided that I should do two things. One, I should talk with my father about scribes who might be available, and two, I should get busy and prepare for my classes. It was almost time for lunch, and I headed for home with a definite bounce to my gait. Mother was already preparing lunch, and she expected father anytime. I said, "Mother, let me help you, and I want you to sit down long enough to read this letter from Sharmila."

"I see now why you have a big smile," she said. "However, I have a question. How will we put up with you while you are waiting?"

"I will not bother anyone. I will be busy. I want to start preparing for my classes."

"That is a good idea, but it could be difficult for you to concentrate on your preparations. An image of Sharmila may surround you and cloud your vision."

"I was about to disagree with you, but, even though you are teasing, you may be right. Either way, I will be occupied."

Just then father came in the door, saying, "I am glad to hear that you will be 'occupied.' But what will you be occupied with?"

"With either class preparations or dreams."

"Dreams," father mused. "Perhaps you are dreaming of Sharmila. Correct?"

"Correct. But how did you know?"

"I could carry on this deception, but the fact is that today I received a letter from Abdi-anati. He said that Sharmila had written to you, and that she would be coming with him to Jerusalem."

"There are no secrets," mother said.

"So, you also know that they will be looking for a scribe," I said. "I had planned to tell you about that."

"Yes. I know, and I will look for some one in the next few days."

We had a good lunch, and the teasing did not cease.

3

WHILE WORKING ON MY class preparations, I had a difficult time concentrating. But I knew I must get started so I could be free when Sharmila arrived. I did not have to prepare for my beginning Egyptian class. Khety, our teacher from Egypt, asked me to teach this a few years ago, and I have taught it several times. Khety wanted to spend more time with advanced students. But I did have to work on my second class. This class would be about story telling. I was going to look at some of the stories in *The Royal Epic* and compare them with Egyptian stories that were told for entertainment. The Egyptian stories were: *The Story of Sinuhe, The Story of the Shipwrecked Sailor, The Enchanted Prince,* and *The Story of Wenamon.* These stories all have a common theme: the wanderings of a hero, and they are climaxed with a joyous homecoming. Khety brought the texts of these stories from Egypt. However the ending of the text of *The Enchanted Prince* has been lost. Khety gave me some suggestions for writing an ending for this story. He said that the most important thing about the ending was to be sure that the hero got back to his homeland before his death, because he had to be buried in Egypt. Also we did not have a good text of *The Story of Wenamon;* it was damaged in transit. But we knew that if we could not figure it out, we would get another text. *The Story of Wenamon* was a recent tale compared to the others. It was about a hundred years old, and it was probably based on an actual report. I was drawn to it, because most of the events happened not far from here along the coast of the Great Sea. Furthermore, I immediately began to plan my visit to the places that are mentioned in this wonderful story.

I worked on my translations of these stories, but finally I had to quit. I kept thinking about Sharmila. I was convinced that I had always loved her, and I was certain that these feelings were not new and were not surfacing just because Rachel had fallen in love with Samuel. I decided to start planning for what we could do when Sharmila and her father arrived. Mother had already told me they could stay at our house, and that meant there would be some good times around our table. But we needed to do some other things.

I did not know how long they would stay, but I planned for several days. On the first day, I would show her around Jerusalem. The next day, I thought we should walk to Bethlehem. On the third day, I wanted to visit the estate of Tamar and Khety. But as soon as I thought about that I changed my mind, saying to myself, "No. I will ask Tamar and Khety if I can go to their place and meet Sharmila before she and her father arrive in Jerusalem."

I could not wait. I went to Khety's office, so I could ask him as soon as possible. Khety was in his office eating his lunch. He said, "*Shalom.* Come in and join me. I will even give you a bit of bread and cheese. I'm eating in my office, because Tamar left this morning for her old home. She wanted to check on her garden. The student, who lives there, does a fair job in tending to things, but Tamar likes to do a little extra now and then."

"I don't need to eat now. I will be going home soon, but I do have a question for you."

"You may be going home for lunch, but this is a special bread and cheese. Tamar is an artist; her food is always prepared with one thing in mind: to please the palate."

"And you are an artist with words. How can I refuse?"

The bread and the cheese were delicious. I enjoyed eating and being with Khety. He was always a lot of fun. I wondered if all Egyptians were like him. Then I told him that I was working on my translations of the stories. Then I said, "I have finished my translation of *The Enchanted Prince*. I even wrote an ending. Could I show it to you in a few days?"

"Of course. Bring it by any time."

"Also I have a request. A few years ago when we went to Beth-shan, you teased me about being smitten by Abdi-anati's daughter, Sharmila."

"I remember her well. Beautiful. Beyond compare."

"I thought you would remember. In a few days, she will be coming to Jerusalem with her father. I would like to meet them at Tamar's estate before they arrive in Jerusalem. Could you ask Tamar if that would be possible?"

"I will ask her this evening. Come by the house just after sunset. But I should give you a warning. You will be meeting Sharmila at Tamar's estate, and as you know that is where Tamar and I fell in love and decided to marry. It is a dangerous location. It is just far enough north of Jerusalem to cut out the city noise. The sky is clear; the stars are bright. You will have to watch your step," Khety said all of this with that mischievous twinkle in his eyes.

"I like danger and adventure, and I thank you for the bread, for the cheese, for the warning, and for being my teacher and my friend."

"Not a word. See us this evening."

4

DURING OUR EVENING MEAL, father said, "Today I received another letter from Abdi-anati. Naam, you will be interested in knowing that he is bringing his wife and both daughters. He has also been corresponding with Sheva, as the head of the academy, about this trip. Sarah and Sheva have invited Abdi-anati and his family to stay at their estate, which as you know is next to Tamar and Khety's place. Also, Keziah, you will not have to make room for them here."

"That does call for some big changes," said mother. "But we will still have them for some meals, and I should talk with Sarah. We will probably do something at their country place."

"Changes indeed," I said. "I was going over to Tamar and Khety's after dinner to ask them if I could meet Sharmila and her father at their place before they arrived in Jerusalem. Since both places are side by side, I could still meet the family when they reach Sheva and Sarah's."

"You seem to be anxious," father said.

Mother's comment was, "Jonathan, you know he is anxious. Naam, you should go on over to see Tamar and Khety. Elissa and Ruth, your dear sisters, will take on your after-dinner chores this evening. I can see that everyone is getting involved in this visit."

I left at once. I knew that the girls would complain about the extra work but not for long.

I ran across the street to Tamar and Khety's house. Khety greeted me with a cup of wine and said, "Sit down here at the table. We have finished eating, but we are still enjoying our wine."

As I sat down Tamar said, "Khety told me about your request, and we want you to know that you are more than welcome to go out to the house to meet Sharmila and her father."

"I thank you. I want to do this, but I have to tell you the situation is going to be different from what I thought. Father just told us that according to a letter he received today, Abdi-anati is bringing his wife and both girls.

They have accepted an invitation from Sheva and Sarah to stay at their estate. I would still like to go to your place and wait for them. I can help them get settled at Sheva and Sarah's."

"That would be fine, said Tamar. "In addition, I think we should plan a party at our place while they are here. There is enough room with both houses for all of us to stay over night. I will have to talk with Keziah and Sarah. We will make some plans."

"Sounds good," I said.

Then Khety inquired, "Naam, do you remember Sharmila's sister's name? Their mother's name is Pidray."

"Her name is Huraya, but when we were there I did not get to talk with her. She is younger than Sharmila. She will be able to have a good time with my sisters. Elissa is now sixteen; Ruth is thirteen; and I think Huraya is also sixteen"

"But if Huraya spends her time with your sisters, Sharmila will be all alone," Khety said.

"She won't be alone. But the question is: can we be alone?"

I finished my wine, and I left after a few moments. As I was leaving, Khety reminded me to bring my translation of *The Enchanted Prince* to his office.

"I will bring it in the morning," I said. "See you then."

With that we said good night.

5

IN A FEW DAYS father received one more letter from Abdi-anati telling us when our friends from Beth-shan would arrive. I left Jerusalem one day before they were expected, and I went to Tamar and Khety's estate. It was north of Jerusalem and just south of Gibeah where Saul had lived. I left after breakfast, and it was still in the cool of the morning when I arrived. Joel, the student who looked after things, greeted me. I recognized him immediately as I had seen him several times at the academy. I asked if there was anything I could do to help. He said that I could help him weed part of the garden, and after that we would go up the road to Sheva's place and help his friend Jacob get ready for the guests. I thought it was a great plan.

"Just show me where to start weeding, and we will get this done."

"Follow me. I'll show you where to start, and I will do some watering."

As we were walking along the path, I said, "Joel, do you like living here better than in the city?"

"Yes. The city is important, as is the academy for our work, but this country is so beautiful, so quiet; it is full of flowers and birds. I have to prepare my own food, but during the growing season it is fresh. Yes. I like it. Also, I like being away from the stress and conflict in the academy. There are students who are really searching for truth, but there are many who really do not care about anything. Well, here we are."

Joel got me started. I had helped Tamar when I was younger, and I knew what I was expected to do. As I worked I thought about what Joel had said. There were students who should not be in the academy. Some of them were there in order to be on their own. They liked what the city had to offer; they liked the willing women among other things. But enough of that, I really did like being here. It was good to have my hands in the dirt. We finished our work about noon. We did not take time for a sit-down lunch. We grabbed some bread and cheese and walked over to see Jacob. He was busy cleaning up the house. He suggested that we could help by cleaning up the yard.

Sheva and Sara's place needed a lot of work. At one time the property belonged to Joab, and it appeared that he had done very little to keep it up. Joab was known to everyone around this area as an evil person. He had tried to rape my mother, and he killed my grandfather, Gad. David did the right thing when he took this royal land grant away from Joab and gave it to Sheva and Sarah.

Joel and I started by re-stacking the rock walls on either side of the entrance gate to the house yard. The walls had fallen down, and the rocks were scattered and some were missing. When we finished, it looked much better. We also pruned a tree in the yard, and I found the makings for a bench. A nice tree needs a bench.

"Joel," I said. "I think we should be getting ready for our guests. I will go in the house and help Jacob find something for dinner, and you could go back to Tamar's garden and get some fresh cucumbers and other vegetables. I would like to have something ready for our travelers."

"Fine. I'll be right back."

I went in the house and spoke to Jacob. "What do you have that we can fix for our friends to eat?"

"We have bread, cheese, yogurt, and honey."

"Joel is going to bring some garden things. I think we have cleaned enough for today. We should get the table and the food ready."

When Joel returned, he and Jacob got things ready. I went up to the spring and cleaned it out. I let it run just a bit until it was clear. Then I filled several jugs with water and carried them to the house.

We were ready. I told my new friends to rest while I walked up the road to meet our guests. I did not walk far deciding instead to sit on a rock and wait for them. Of course, they might be late. If so I would just have to go back to the house and hope they would get here the following day. But there was still time. Sitting on one rock, I leaned against a larger one. As I looked up, I watched the graceful flight of an eagle. I thought about the old Egyptian tale of *The Enchanted Prince* that I had just translated. The Prince could fly, and I thought about how everyone, who has ever watched an eagle fly, surely has dreamed of flying. Eagles fly with such ease. Just then I heard something. I quit dreaming about flying and stood up. Someone was coming down the road. I started walking toward the sound. Sharmila spotted me, and she came running. She reached for my hands, and I drew her to me and kissed her.

"It is wonderful to see you," I said. "However, if I remember correctly, after a long trip Rebekah saw Isaac walking toward her, and she promptly put on her veil. But you found a place in my arms."

"Yes I did, and I remember that Jacob kissed Rachel when he first met her."

"That he did."

So I kissed her again, but it was a short one. The rest of the party was fast approaching.

I greeted Abdi-anati and his wife, Pidray, and Sharmila's sister Huraya. They looked tired. "This has been a long trip for you," I said. "You did not have the king's mules as we did when we visited you."

"No," answered Abdi-anati. "But these three donkeys were a great help. As you see, one of them carried our things, and the other two were available for anyone who was tired of walking. But it was a long trip; it took us four days."

"And we made the trip in two days with the mules," I said. "Now we will get on to the house. We have some food ready, and you will be able to eat and rest. It is just around the next bend."

We were soon there. After the introductions, I asked Joel to take the donkeys over to Tamar's small pasture. We were not sure about the pastures here at Sheva's place. They might not be stock-tight. Jacob helped me set out the food, and Pidray and her girls added some things to our table. Sharmila said that she brought a melon just for me, and perhaps after dinner we could eat it outside in the yard. We had a good dinner and a good time. I got to know Pidray and Huraya much better. It was obvious that Huraya was a lot of fun and this did not go unnoticed by Joel and Jacob. She also teased Sharmila.

She said to me, "Sharmila has been difficult to live with on this trip. She thinks you will be anxious to see her. I have told her not to expect too much."

"I don't want to question your wisdom, but I was anxious and full of expectations." I said this and noticed that Sharmila was blushing as she shook her fist at Huraya.

Everyone was tired, but they were also delighted to be in our cool thin air. Pidray said, "At home it would still be muggy and hot."

All of us helped to clean up and put the food away. After that we showed our guests their sleeping quarters. I said, "Joel, Jacob, and I will be across the road at Tamar's, and you should all sleep late."

Abdi-anati said, "We never sleep late; we enjoy the cool of the mornings."

And Pidray added, "I will want to bake some bread. Jacob, before you leave show me your fire pit and oven."

Sharmila got her melon, and we went out to the bench in the front yard. She said, "The first time I spoke to you, I served you a slice of melon. I thought this would bring back some of those first feelings."

"You had some 'first feelings'? I thought I was the one with the 'first feelings.' In fact, your beauty caused a lump in my throat or rather a pain; I could not speak for a moment."

"I thought you were just bashful. I was serving you the melon, and I was interested in the notes you were taking during my father's conversation with Khety and your father. But I was also interested in talking with you, and yes, I did have some strange feelings. These feelings were repeated a few years ago when we met in Jerusalem, but I never said much about them in the few letters I wrote."

"Perhaps we were both too busy to write much, but I have never forgotten you. When you were here before, I remember that you met Rachel."

"Yes. And I was always certain that you would marry her."

"That is what most people thought, but Rachel and I have both realized that we are like siblings. By the way, she will marry a fine student by the name of Samuel. She told me that when she met Samuel she could not understand the feeling; she called it love. That is when I knew that my feelings for you should be called love, but I was afraid. I thought, 'Sharmila has probably met a "Samuel" by now.' That is why I wrote, and when I received your letter, I shouted for joy."

"What you didn't understand is that I had already met my 'Samuel,' and his name is Naam, and I love him."

With that I took her into my arms, and we kissed.

"Perhaps the melon was not needed," she said, "but I brought it all the way from Beth-shan. We should eat the melon."

"That old familiar pain is in my throat, and I think I need some melon."

We kissed again, and we both ate; from the same piece of melon we ate.

"My throat is better. The melon helped."

"Are you sure it was the melon?"

"I am only sure of one thing: you are beyond compare, and as the sages would say, 'your worth is far beyond that of rubies.' I suggest that we take the rest of the melon in the house for your folks, and I will see you in the morning."

6

Joel, Jacob, and I got up early, and we worked for a time in Tamar's garden. From across the road, we could also smell Pidray's bread baking. It did not take long for us to agree to follow the aroma to its source. As we entered the courtyard Abdi-anati welcomed us, saying to me, "As soon as we have had something to eat, we should leave for Jerusalem. I want to talk with your father today. Joel and Jacob can stay and help Pidray fix a few things around here. Huraya will stay and help her mother, and I know that Sharmila will want to come with us."

"That sounds like a great plan."

"I thought you would like it."

"I do, but I need to talk with your wife about some other plans."

I went into the house and spoke with Pidray. "My mother, Keziah, Tamar, and Sarah want to have a party out here for you and your family. When I return this evening, I will be able to tell you when it will be. Right now I am guessing it will be in two days, but I can tell you for certain tonight. They will bring lots of food. In the meantime, you should feel free to use Tamar's garden."

"Thank you. I will be glad to meet the others. Now, you should call everyone, and we will eat."

Before I left the house, I met Sharmila near the door. We looked at each other but did not kiss. She asked me if my throat felt better. I said, "I think it is worse."

Then I called the others in for breakfast. Abdi-anati, Sharmila, and I finished first. We were ready to go to Jerusalem, so Sharmila and I went out to the road but we had to wait a few moments for Abdi-anati to gather up some documents and put them in his pack. So I confessed to Sharmila, "I really don't know what to do. You have said that you loved me, and I love you. I want to marry you, but how will it work out? When? Where? And should I keep my feelings for you from your family?"

"My family knows about our feelings for each other. They have known for some time, and their knowledge was confirmed last night by our happy faces. As to your questions, I also want to marry but don't worry. We will figure it out. We were both fourteen when we met at Beth-shan. That was six years ago. We can take a few more days to make our plans. In the meantime, let's enjoy our time together on our walk this morning. My father will not object if you hold my hand."

"And let me add that my family also knows that I am in love with you. It will be great to show our smiling faces to them as well."

We had a nice walk, and when we arrived in Jerusalem, I took Abdianati directly to father's office. Then Sharmila and I went to the house to see mother.

Mother was home, expecting us, but Elissa and Ruth were disappointed that Huraya was not with us. Mother sighed, "Don't worry girls. You will get to meet her in two days."

Mother embraced Sharmila and asked her about her mother and sister. Sharmila said that everyone enjoyed the trip, and they were impressed with the accommodations. Looking at her lovingly, mother said, "I hope that two days will give everyone enough rest, and that you will all be ready for our party."

"Everyone will be rested, and we will look forward to it," Sharmila assured her.

Mother continued, "You both look like you are having a good time. You should sit down at the table, and we will try some of Elissa's raisin cakes."

"Since we ate early this morning, this is just what I need," I said. "And mother, you have always had a sharp eye. Sharmila and I are having a great time. In fact, I know that these next few days are going to be precious, but they will be gone faster than the morning dew."

"True," said Sharmila. "But remember the morning dew is essential for growth and maturity."

"Right. That works for the grapes, but for me I don't know. I'll try to be positive. Mother, I want to show Sharmila around Jerusalem. We will be back in time for lunch. And Elissa, thanks for the treats."

"You are welcome, my dear brother, and I am willing to help you show Sharmila around Jerusalem."

"That will not be necessary, my dear sister."

Sharmila added her thanks, and we left hand-in-hand. After taking a quick look at David's palace, Sharmila asked, "Can we climb that hill just to the east? I would like to find a nice place to sit, and we could just view the city from up there."

I agreed to her plan, and it did not take long. We walked down by the Gihon spring and into the valley. It did not take long to climb to the top of the ridge, and looking west the view was magnificent.

"Good idea," I said. "I get caught up in the city and in my work. I do not come up here for the overview, as I should. Because of my studies, I know we are surrounded by a big world, but I need to see it. Magon, our teacher from Tyre, says that the world seems bigger when you live by the Great Sea."

"He is right. I have been to Tyre with my father, and I had a similar experience."

"So, it is good to be reminded of our world, but right now I would rather look at the most important person in my world. Sharmila, you are not only gorgeous, but you are thoughtful. I don't know how I have lived without you."

"And you, my dear Naam, are like your father and my father; you talk too much."

She came to me, and we enjoyed being close and silent.

On our way back to the academy and to mother's lunch, I said, "I don't know if I can take it if you go back to Beth-shan with your family. I would go with you, but I have these two courses to teach at the academy."

"Perhaps I could stay here. I need to talk to my parents about this. If father finds a scribe or two, I would not be needed."

"But if you stay here, we should get married. I want you and need you."

"I know," and with a smile she said, "And in that order."

We had a good time at lunch. Elissa and Ruth talked with Sharmila. Magon, Khety, Abdi-anati, and father were all there. I helped mother get things ready.

Abdi-anati was saying, "Jonathan, when you and Khety were in Beth-shan six years ago, I told you that we needed some help from David. I explained that all the Egyptian mercenaries from Caphtor (Crete) and Alashiya (Cyprus)—who had ruled us for ages—had fled before David became king, and they joined with the Philistines. We needed leadership for our city to function, and we needed some protection. You said that you would speak with David, and he sent us some assistance. Things are much better, and I want to thank you."

"It is good to know that things are better, father said. "But now you need more scribes. I suppose that a closer relationship with Jerusalem has created some of that need."

"Correct, but in addition you, Magon, and Khety have inspired me to do some other work. I have tried to locate more Egyptian material, and I am gathering some tales about our city. As you well know there are so many things to write about. Sharmila has helped me, but I really need two more scribes."

We all sat down to eat. Magon remembered Abdi-anati from when Abdi-anati was in school at Tyre. They had a lot to talk about, and Khety, as always was interested in any new Egyptian material. Sharmila and I talked with mother, and I think we were both relieved not to have to think about our own problem for a few moments.

After lunch Abdi-anati left to interview some students, and Khety announced that we would all be together again in just two days at the party. "We have two houses," he said. "We expect for you to be able to stay over night."

Mother said to Sharmila and me, "I must speak with Tamar, Naomi, and Sarah about our plans."

"I'm sorry," said Sharmila. "I don't know Naomi."

"She is one of my best friends; she is Magon's wife. They have two children, a son Azriel and a daughter Ahinoam. I also think Elishama and Deborah will come to the party. I believe that you have met their daughter Rachel, and they also have Joshua and Dinah."

"I have met Rachel. This sounds like fun. There will be a lot of people."

"Right, and I think Naam and you should see Rachel and Samuel before you leave this afternoon. You should give them a special invitation. Naam, would you agree?"

"It is fine with me if Sharmila agrees."

"I would like that. We should see them here and not wait until the party."

The girls were busy and the others had left. I took Sharmila's hand, and said to mother, "We have been in love for a long time, and we can finally say it."

"I'm happy for you, and it was apparent when you arrived. Now you go along and find Rachel and Samuel."

This was an easy task. We found them at Rachel's where they were still having lunch. Things seemed just a little tense at first, but eased when I invited them to the party. I said, "We thought you would be there with the rest of your family, but we just wanted to make sure that you came along. Sharmila and I want to get married soon, and I suppose that the two of you have had some of the same thoughts. We would like to know about some of your plans. Also I imagine that we will all be connected to the academy in the next few years, and that means we have a lot in common."

"We will be there," Rachel said. "Sharmila, I want to get to know you, and both you and Naam need to know more about Samuel."

"I'm glad you stopped by," said Samuel. "I really did not know just what we should do."

"We will have a great time," said Sharmila. "I can see that there will be enough young people there to keep the party lively."

As we left Sharmila remarked that she was glad we had given them a special invitation. She said, "Your mother has a lot of good ideas."

"She does, and I think it is because she is always thinking about the well-being of others."

7

ABDI-ANATI CAME BACK TO the house to tell us that he would need to stay at the academy for more interviews. He suggested that Sharmila and I go back without him, saying that he would come with the other men to the party.

Mother packed us a snack for our walk back to Tamar's, and when we sat down to eat it, I said, "I am wondering if we could get married on the second day of the party. All the Jerusalem folks would be returning on that day, and we could have Tamar's house for our wedding night."

Sharmila kissed me saying, "I would like that, and it might be the best time. However, I will have to talk with mother about this. Also could you get word to your mother about our plans? She would want to think about what she would need for a wedding."

"You are right. Joel and Jacob will probably be going to Jerusalem tomorrow, and I could send a letter with them. If not I will go back tomorrow morning. You need to talk with your mother this evening."

"I will."

"And we also need make a few plans. In my mind, our wedding started with your journey the other day. Your journey was the wedding procession. My father always called Rebekah's journey a wedding procession. Of course, as we know, at the end of your procession you did not veil yourself for your "Isaac."

"No! I did not, but your arms held me, and your kiss was what I had been waiting for."

"So since our wedding has already started, we will have to finish it. On the second day of the party, the others can bring you to Tamar's house."

"That won't take long."

"No, but the women will have to party at Sarah's and the men will be at Tamar's. That will take some time."

As soon as we arrived, Sharmila talked with her mother. Pidray was not surprised, and confided that she had brought some clothes for Sharmila in case there was a wedding. Sharmila said, "How did you know?"

Pidray drew her daughter into her arms and said, "I know my girl. It was written in your eyes and in your smile. Your heart is an open book."

They both had tears on their cheeks when they came out of the house and told me to start writing my letter to mother.

"That I can do," I said.

Running to the bench under the tree, I began to write.

After writing about half of the letter, I looked up and saw mother with my two sisters standing at the gate. I almost fell off of the bench. "What a surprise! I was just writing a letter to you. I was going to send it down to you with Jacob or Joel."

"Well now you can just tell me your news. On second thought you don't have to tell me. I can guess what you were writing. You were telling me that our party will include a wedding. Right?"

"How did you know?"

"It was obvious. I just looked at the two of you, and I thought that you could not say good-bye again. So, here we are. We brought along some extra things for the wedding. We will have a day before the others arrive. Now I want to meet Sharmila's mother."

I took mother and the girls into the house. Sharmila couldn't believe her eyes. She ran to mother for a big hug. Mother said, "I want to meet your mother, and I see by your happy tears that you have been talking about something important."

Sharmila turned to her mother and said, "Mother this is Keziah, Naam's mother."

"And you are Pidray. I am happy to meet you."

I said, "I was writing my letter, and I looked up; there they were. My mother had guessed that there would be a wedding and decided to come early. Perhaps she senses these things because her father was a prophet."

"No," said Pidray. "We just know our children. She did not need to guess."

After all of this my sisters, Elissa and Ruth, already had introduced themselves to Huraya, and the three of them ran outside to plan their activities.

"We will get them to help us after we know what we need to do," said mother. "However, it is getting late, and we won't get much done today. But we have tomorrow, and the rest of the women and children will be here the next morning. I don't expect the men until later. Sharmila and Naam, you had better take a walk and catch your breath. I will help Pidray with supper, which she started before the two of you interrupted her preparations."

Sharmila and I went out side and walked over to Tamar's. We sat on one of the terrace walls in the garden. We were both praising our mothers' intuitions and their willingness to help. I said, "We thought this was going to be a big problem, but everything just fell into place."

"Our mothers are sensitive and in touch. We should have known that they would help us. I am happy, and soon we will really be together."

As I kissed her I said, "I can't wait for that moment."

"I think we can wait, but perhaps not, if you keep kissing me like that, and it is getting dark. We should invite Joel and Jacob for supper and walk back."

When we got back to the house our supper was ready. In fact the girls were already eating, and mother and Pidray were getting to know each other and having a friendly conversation. We sat down at the table, and the girls began to tease us. But as soon as Jacob and Joel came in their attention was turned to them. Mother and Pidray made some remark about getting some food ready for the "love birds."

The next day everyone had a job, but we also had a lot of fun. We cleaned both houses and both yards. Joel helped us with the work, but Jacob had to go to Jerusalem, and he was instructed to tell Sarah and Tamar about the wedding. In the afternoon we all helped mother and Pidray with a lot of baking and cooking. Joel and I gathered wood, carried water, and brought onions and herbs from Tamar's garden. By evening we were all tired. I did not sleep much because I was too excited, and I wanted to write something for Sharmila.

In the morning the women from the academy arrived early. This was the first day of the party. Sarah, Tamar, Deborah, and Naomi came with the children, and everyone carried some of the supplies. They wanted to get things ready, and Sarah said, "The men will be here later; they claimed that they had work to finish. We left some heavier things for them to bring. Jonathan said he would bring a donkey to carry the wine."

"That sounds like a good idea," mother said.

Everyone was introduced to Pidray and Huraya. The new arrivals were ready for rest before they started their preparations. Sarah said, "We were told yesterday that there was going to be a wedding. Is that the case?"

"That is right," said mother. "I came a day early, because I just thought that this might happen."

"Keziah has always been correct about such things," said Naomi. "She knew that Magon and I would marry, and she also knew that Tamar and Khety had wedding plans."

Rachel and Samuel came immediately to Sharmila and me, and Rachel said to Sharmila, "I am jealous. I thought Samuel and I would have our wedding first, but we will have to wait until Samuel's folks can come to Jerusalem."

"My folks will be leaving in two days for Beth-shan. We had to do this now," said Sharmila.

"I suppose so, but I thought that Naam must have pressured you for a quick marriage."

"No. It may have been the other way around."

Then I said with ironic denial, "I hate to interrupt your conversation, but we did not pressure each other. Yes, we were under pressure, but it was as if we had a fever. It may have been those mosquitoes at Beth-shan or some love-bug."

Rachel said with Samuel smiling, "I don't believe a word of that, but we are happy for you."

Rachel and Sharmila hugged, and Samuel said to me, "Those two are going to have a good time in the years to come."

8

IT LOOKS LIKE THIS is going to be a long book. I did not plan to give so many details leading up to our marriage, but the story has a way of taking over.

So, the party was fun for all of us. The men arrived in time for lunch, which I am sure was no coincidence. Jacob and his friend Joseph were with them. Jacob and Joseph had decided to go to Beth-shan to work for Abdi-anati. All the men were eager to sit down at the long table that we had constructed under the tree. I don't think the children ever sat down for lunch, but they had been snatching a bite here and there as the food was being put on the table. But the adults all sat down and enjoyed the great picnic. We had bread, several kinds of cheese, honey, cold lamb, yogurt, sliced cucumbers from Tamar's garden, raisin cakes, and wine. Before we began to eat, Khety stood up and said, "As you know, I am from Egypt, and today we have guests from Beth-shan. The Egyptians ruled Beth-shan for many years, and people of Beth-shan acquired some Egyptian tastes. Hence the people from Egypt and Beth-shan love their beer. So for this great occasion I have made some beer, and I hope you all enjoy it."

Everyone gave Khety a cheer, and Pidray announced that for our evening meal we would have her lamb stew along with Khety's beer and after dinner some melon from Beth-shan. Everyone had plenty to eat; some of the folks looked sleepy, but the conversation was too rich and kept the sleepy ones from nodding.

At one point father said, "King Saul's capital was at Gibeah, which is only a short walk north of where we are sitting. I suppose that these two estates furnished a lot of food for Saul's table in the past."

"But it was probably not prepared like our food today," said Khety. "This was really fine."

Tamar added, "It is also much more peaceful around here than it was in the days of Saul, and I want all of you to know that when David removed Joab from this property and gave it to Sheva and Sarah, Khety and I felt so much safer at our place."

"I'm sure you did," said mother. "I hope we never see Joab again."

Khety said, "I am changing the subject, but I understand that to-morrow we are having a wedding. In Beth-shan a few years ago, we were learned that the name Sharmila means 'alabaster.' Today I remembered that in Egyptian we have two words that are important for this occasion. They are similar words with separate meanings, but they are related to this event. Note the following:

Egyptian Šs (*Shes*) = alabaster = Sharmila

Egyptian Sš (*Sesh*) = scribe = Naam and Sharmila

I think these two belong together, and tomorrow will be their day."

Everyone gave us a big cheer. I said to the group, "Sharmila and I understand that our marriage started with her trip or procession from Beth-shan to Jerusalem. For that reason the procession tomorrow will be very short, like just across the road. And since Khety has changed the subject to our wedding and alabaster, I want to read a short poem:

> Sharmila, the stone of preference,
> Sculptors delight in this fine white stone.
> Of fine alabaster, she is a work of art.
> My Sharmila is real;
> She is beautiful.
> The sculptors can come close,
> But there is that ever-present gap
> Between the person and the image,
> Between the reality and the appearance.
> This is true for art and for our lives.
> In our lives we will attempt to narrow
> The gap between our hopes and ideas
> And the persons who appear before you;
> We mean to be truthful.

Sharmila got up and ran to me; she gave me a short thank-you kiss. Samuel said, "Not fair! Save the kissing for after she crosses the road."

Everyone laughed, and the good times continued. Rachel, Samuel, Sharmila, and I went for a walk on the road. We walked north toward Gibeah, and we had a wonderful time just being together.

Later mother told me that after we left the conversation changed in tone. My father warned the others about a shift in David's view of his kingship.

Father said, "Tamar, David helped you, and he has helped most of us who are sitting around this table. He has also made some bad decisions for us. Nevertheless, David has a kind heart, and he loves his children more than most fathers. But I am worried about his present view of his kingship. I don't worry that it will change him at this stage of his rule, but it could change the way in which his successor views the kingship."

"Have you talked to him recently?" asked Sheva.

"Yes, but we did not discuss his views on his position as king. However, he did give me a poem, which he referred to as his *Last Words*. These may not be his last words, but I have a copy of it. I hesitate to change the mood of our party, but I want read it for you:

> The oracle of David son of Jesse,
> The oracle of the hero, who was exalted,
> The anointed of the God of Jacob,
> The singer of the heroic songs of Israel,
> The spirit of Yahweh has spoken through me;
> His words are on my tongue.
> The God of Israel has spoken;
> The Rock of Israel has said to me:
> "He who rules humans righteously,
> He who rules with the fear of God
> Is like the light of morning at sunrise,
> [Like] a morning without clouds,
> [Or like] brightness after a rain [sprouting] grass from the earth.
> Is not my house right with God?
> For he has made an eternal covenant with me.
> It is arranged in all matters, and it is guarded.
> Will he not make possible my every deliverance
> And my every delight?
> But the wicked with thorns are swept away, all of them,
> For they cannot be picked up by hand;
> Whoever touches them must be armed with iron
> And the shaft of a spear.
> And in the fire they are completely burned in place.
> (2 Samuel 23:1–7)

I must say that this poem worries me."

"It worries me as well," said Sheva, "but Jonathan, please explain for us your worries."

"I will be the historian at this point for those of you who were not with us for David's first and second coronations. After reading David's *Last*

Words, I re-read Keziah's accounts of these coronations in *The Jerusalem Academy*. For the first coronation, David wrote a psalm that most of us thought was not good. For the second coronation, David wrote a much better psalm (Psalm 2). We were all interested in the fact that he was anointed as our king in Hebron, and yet in the psalm he said, 'But I, yes I, have been anointed his king, / On Zion, his holy mountain. / Let me recite the decree of Yahweh. / He said to me, "You are my son . . ."' Zion was our clue that we would be moving to Jerusalem and Mt. Zion. We did not think much about the fact that he claimed to be God's son. After all, most of the heroes of old claimed to be part divine. In the covenant with the House of Saul that Sheva wrote for the second coronation, he mentioned again the decree and that David was God's son, but he also spoke of the decree as being a conditional covenant by adding: 'If your sons keep my covenant and my stipulations, they will sit upon your throne.' This was also stated in great detail in Ahban's psalm (Psalm 132), which was used when David brought the Ark of Yahweh to Jerusalem. Enough history. In David's *Last Words*, he does not speak of a conditional covenant but rather an *eternal covenant*. Now we know that *eternal covenants* are not always eternal. In fact, Joab was given this land where we are now sitting in a royal land grant *forever and forever*. But that means nothing if Joab turns out to be a person of questionable behavior. Nevertheless, in David's *Last Words*, the *eternal covenant* will be interpreted by his successors to be eternal regardless of their behavior.

"I have other complaints. David designates his words as an *oracle*. It seems to me that he has not only taken over the role of the prophet in that he claims that God speaks through him, but unlike the prophet who gives the *oracle of Yahweh*, he gives us the *oracle of David*. This is too much. He is also certain that if he is righteous and fears God, all will go well. He is repeating the false ideas found in *The Story of the Ancient Job*. The fact that *Job II* or *The Rebel Job* argued against these ideas is never even considered. Being righteous and fearing God does not mean that all will be well."

Magon said, "*The Last Words* is a troublesome poem. He exalts himself and the kingship. I guess we can hope that his successor will not read it or rule according to it. It is one thing to be God's shepherd and lead the people, but in this poem the king seems to act and speak as God, not for God but as God."

"He sounds like a Pharaoh," said Khety.

"Right," said Sheva, "We will have to watch this with care, and especially when David gets close to the end of his reign."

"I thought you all needed to know about this," said father. "Now we should get back into our party mood, because I see that the lovers and friends have returned."

9

THE FIVE YOUNGER CHILDREN had a great afternoon. I do not know exactly what they did, but when it was time for our evening meal they were ready to sit and rest for a while.

Before we started eating, Khety stood up and said, "I want the children to know that I have a story for them. I will start the story at the end of our meal when we are served some of Pidray's melon from Beth-shan. If I start it while we are eating the melon, the adults will be able to listen as well without having to admit they still like children's stories."

True to his word, Khety stood as the melon was served. He said, "This is a short story, but I am not going to tell it by memory. I will read it for two reasons: 1) the ending of this Egyptian story has been lost, and 2) I have a new translation of the Egyptian text into your language, and Naam, the translator, has written an ending for us. After you hear the story, you can, with Naam's permission, suggest another ending. One other note: when Egyptian writers or storytellers mention an important person, place, or a God they follow the name with three words, 'life, prosperity, health.' As storytellers, we usually give you the first letter of each word. So, I will just say, 'l.p.h.' "

I did not know that Khety was going to read this, but it sounded like fun. And Khety's reading was always a treat. He had a different voice for every character. So he started:

THE ENCHANTED PRINCE

Let it be known that there was once a king who did not have a son. After a while his Majesty, l.p.h., requested from the local gods a son for himself. They commanded that one should be born for him. During that night he slept with his wife, and yes, she became pregnant. After she completed her months for childbearing, a son was born, and the Hathors, those goddesses who determine the fate of newborns, came to appoint for him a fate. They said, "He will die by the crocodile, or the serpent, or even the dog."

When the people who were with the child heard this, they repeated it to his Majesty, l.p.h. Then his Majesty, l.p.h., became very sad in his heart. So his Majesty, l.p.h., had a house of stone built for his son out in the desert, and he equipped it with people and with every good thing of the king's palace, l.p.h. The child did not go outside anywhere.

After the child had grown older, he went up to the roof of his castle, and he saw a greyhound; it was following an old man who was walking on the road. He said to his servant, who was beside him, "What is that walking behind the old man who is coming on the road?"

He told him, "That is a greyhound."

The child said to him, "Bring one just like it to me."

Then the servant went to report it to his Majesty, l.p.h. His Majesty, l.p.h., said, "Bring for him a frisky puppy, because of the grieving of his heart."

So they brought him the greyhound.

Now after many days had passed beyond this, the child was fully developed in all his body. He sent to his father saying, "For what purpose am I just sitting here? I am committed to the fate. So let me go. I will do according to my heart, and the God will do what is in his heart."

Then they hitched up a chariot, equipped with many weapons. He was given his servant, and he was ferried across to the eastern land. He was told, "Go wherever your heart desires," and his greyhound was with him. He went north into the desert, following his heart and living on the best of all the desert game.

Finally he reached the Prince of the land of Naharin. Now the Prince of the land of Naharin did not father any one except a daughter, an eligible wife, and he built a house for her; its window was far up, seventy cubits from the ground. Then he sent for all the sons of all the princes of the land of Khor, and he told them, "The one who reaches the window of my daughter, she shall be a wife for him."

After many days had passed beyond this and the princes were doing their daily practice, the young man passed by them. They took the young man to their house. They bathed him; they gave feed to his team. They did everything for the young man: they anointed him, they bandaged his feet, they gave food to his servant, and they talked to him, planning to cause him to speak. "Where do you come from, you good-looking lad?"

He said to them, "I am the son of a chariot officer of the land of Egypt. My mother died, and my father took for himself another wife, a stepmother. She came to hate me, and I ran away, fleeing from her presence." The princes embraced him, and they kissed his whole body.

After many days had passed beyond this, he said to the princes, "What is this that you are doing, O princes?"

They said to him, "For three months now, we have been here using this time to practice flying. For the one who reaches the window of the daughter of the Prince of the land of Naharin, he will give her to him for a wife."

Then he said to them, "If I could *enchant my feet*, I would go flying with you."

They went flying according to their daily practice, these princes.

Then the young man stood at a distance watching, and also the daughter of the Prince of the land of Naharin watched him.

Now after some time passed beyond this, the young man came to fly with the sons of the princes. He flew and he reached the window of the daughter of the Prince of the land of Naharin. She kissed him; she embraced his whole body.

Then someone went to take the good news to her father, and said to him, "Someone has reached the window of your daughter."

So the Prince asked him saying, "A son of which of the princes?"

And one said to him, "He is a son of a chariot officer. He came fleeing from the land of Egypt and from the presence of his stepmother."

Then the Prince of the land of Naharin became exceedingly angry. Then he asked, "Am I to give my daughter to this fugitive from Egypt? Send him back."

Someone came and said to him, "You must go back to the place from which you came."

But the daughter seized the young man, and she swore by God saying, "By Pre-Harakhti, if he is taken away from me, I will not eat; I will not drink; I shall die within the hour."

Then the messenger went and reported to her father every word that she had said, her father sent men to slay him right where he was.

The daughter said to them, "By Pre, if they slay him, at the setting of the sun, I shall be dead. I shall not live an hour more than he."

Then someone went to tell her father, and her father had the young man, together with his daughter, brought before him. When the young man came before him, the Prince understood his value. He embraced him, and he kissed his whole body.

He said to him, "Tell me about your story. Note, you have been given to me as a son."

The young man said to him, "I am the son of a chariot officer of the land of Egypt. My mother died, and my father took for himself another wife. She came to hate me, and I ran away, fleeing from her presence."

Then he gave him his daughter for a wife. He gave him a house with fields as well as cattle and all good things.

Now after some time had passed beyond this, the young man said to his wife, "I have been given to three fates: the crocodile, the serpent, or the dog."

Then she said to him, "So, have the dog that follows after you killed."

He said to her, "That is foolishness. I will not have my dog killed, whom I raised from a puppy."

She started to guard her husband with great zeal and did not allow him to go outside walking alone.

Now on the day on which the young man had journeyed from the land of Egypt to wander about, behold the crocodile, his fate, followed him from the land of Egypt. The crocodile came to live in the midst of the lake next to the village where the young man was with his wife. Behold, a giant was in the lake. The giant would not allow the crocodile to come out for walking, and the crocodile would not allow the giant to come out to walk about. When the sun rose, they stood up and fought each other every day for a period of three months.

Now after [many] days had passed beyond this, the young man sat down and made a holiday in his house. After the end of the evening breeze, the young man lay down upon his bed, and sleep overcame his body. Then his wife filled one jar with wine; she filled another jar with beer. Then a serpent came forth from his hole to bite the young man. But his wife was sitting beside him, and she was not sleeping. So she put the jars before the serpent, and he drank and became drunk and then lay down belly up. Next his wife cut it into pieces with her axe. Then they woke her husband, and she said to him, "*Look! Your God has given one of your fates into your hand. He will protect you from your fates.*"

Then he made an offering to Pre, praising him and extolling his might in the course of every day.

Now after many days had passed beyond this, the young man went out to walk for pleasure on his place. His wife did not go out with him, but his dog was following him. Then his dog began to speak, saying, "I am your fate."

Thereupon, he ran from the dog. He reached the lake; he went into the water; he fled from the dog. Then the crocodile seized him, and carried him to the place of the giant. The crocodile told the young man, "I am your fate who was made to come after you, but for three months now I have been fighting with the giant. Now look, I shall release you. If my enemy returns to fight, you shall help me kill the giant. For if you see the giant you will see the crocodile."

Now after the earth had become bright on the next day, the giant returned.

(The text ends here and the rest is the ending by Naam.)

The crocodile called to the young man for help. He came running. The crocodile grabbed the giant's feet in his jaws, and the young man with his enchanted feet flew high. He came down hard on the head of the giant and beat him around his eyes. The giant could not see, and the crocodile held his feet and pulled him back. At the same time the young man flew around and hit the giant in the back. The giant fell forward and drowned. The crocodile was tired, and he had been kicked. Then the crocodile said, "Now I will help you with your dog. He is also your fate as he had proclaimed. The crocodile crawled on to the shore, and he caught the dog, and he carried him to the bottom of the lake. The dog was no more, and the crocodile was never seen again.

When the young man reached home, he told his wife what had happened. She said, "I knew that your God would protect you. Now you are free."

"Yes I am free, and perhaps I shall get another puppy."

The young man made offerings to Pre-Harakhti, and he did not forget the crocodile. He made offerings to the crocodile god, Sobek-Re.

Now after many days had passed beyond this, The Prince of the land of Naharin died. The man said to his wife, "We have had a happy life in this land. Now we must take our children, and we will go back to Egypt. There we will live out our last years, and we will be buried in the black earth and journey to the West where there will be good food, good beer, and good music."

This is it, from its beginning to its end, just like most of it was found in a manuscript.

Everyone gave a cheer as Khety finished the reading. Elissa and Ruth ran up and hugged him. Khety said, "My young friends are the best ever."

My sister, Ruth, said, "Khety, you have always told us great stories, but this is the best one yet. I think we should give you a prize for the voice you used when you spoke for the crocodile."

Everyone agreed, and Pidray brought Khety a piece of melon, saying, "Here is your prize."

While still enjoying his melon, Khety added another word: "Naam and I have seen that in your *Royal Epic* the fathers also have a homecoming and a burial in their native land."

"These stories are old prose stories just like ours," said father. "This is important to me. Also they are interested in entertainment. Tellers of tales want to entertain. It is nice to know that we have more than contracts, ritual documents, and chronologies in our libraries."

No one offered a suggestion for another ending, and Magon said, "The new ending seems to have all of the necessary elements for this kind of an Egyptian story. I think it is a good ending with typical Egyptian phrases and language. One thing that still amazes me is how Hathor appears in so many places. In this story she, or her goddesses, hands out the fates to the newborn. She was also known in Byblos where she was identified with their Ba'alat, and she was known at Ugarit where she was pictured nursing royal sons."

"She did get around as did other Egyptian gods," said Khety. "This story is set in the North Country, in the Land of Hanigalbat or what Egyptians call the Land of Naharin. This was the land of the Hurrians; it was the Mitanni Kingdom. In the story the princess knows a lot about Egyptian religion and all about the fates. As I learned in my scribal school, this is not so strange. It has been reported that in the little town of Nuzi, northeast of Babylon near the mountains, there was a palace with many paintings of Hathor. These paintings are like the ones from *Waset* (Thebes) in the palace of Amen-hotep, and he married two princesses from Hanigalbat or Mitanni. Also, we should note on the occasion of this marriage, which we will celebrate, that the Hurrian women from Naharin had the same rights as the men, and they were not afraid to speak up and do what was needed in any crises. It seems clear that they spoke out about their rights and thus influenced our great reformer, Akh-en-Aton, who ruled in Amarna, to give such rights to Egyptian women. Sharmila take note!"

"I will take note," promised Sharmila. She also had a question for Khety, "Does that little town of Nuzi still exist?"

"No. If I remember correctly, the Assyrians destroyed it about 400 years ago. That would be close to the time of Akh-en-Aton and before the destruction of Ugarit by the Sea Peoples about 200 years ago. At least the princesses who came to Egypt with their many women escaped the take over by the Assyrians. The women from Naharin contributed to our culture."

Mother said, "That was a great story, and it was especially good for this wedding party. Naam has his princess and Sharmila has her prince. Her prince cannot fly, but she should not worry; they will not only be equal, but they will climb to new heights. We all wish for them a happy life together.

10

AFTER LYING AWAKE MOST of the night, I got up early on our wedding day. I walked out to Tamar's garden, and to my surprise, Sharmila was there walking along the paths between the terraces. She saw me and held out her arms. As we embraced, she said, "I didn't get much sleep last night. I could not turn off my mind or my emotions. I walked over here thinking you might be here."

"You thought right, and I had the same problem."

"But I think my problem is more complex than yours. I am happy that this is our wedding day, but I will also hate to see the rest of my family return to Beth-shan."

"That does make it difficult. We will have to visit them often."

"That will help, but it will always be difficult to say good-bye."

"True. I have a hard time with good-byes. We must spend as much time with them as possible today."

As we were kissing, we heard kitchen noise from Sarah's kitchen and decided to go over and join the others. When we arrived there was a lot of shouting and well wishes for a great day. We did have a great day. I think we spent most of the day talking, eating, and dancing. By the time we separated into the women's party at Sarah's and the men's at Tamar's, we really did not need any more food. But we had plenty of wine, and we also had plenty of speeches, at least at the men's party. The plan was that the men would leave me at Tamar's and go over to Sarah's and participate in the blessing of the bride; everyone would participate in the procession, and they would bring Sharmila to me. This would be done in the late afternoon, which would give the folks from Jerusalem time to get home before dark.

At the men's party, my father said some important things: "Naam, you are fortunate indeed to find a beautiful wife, who has been raised in the scribal tradition. She reads, writes, and will help you as she did her father. As your mother wrote in *The Minority Report*, 'The male and the female are equal,' but you should know that in your personal relationship Sharmila's beauty and your desire for her will always subordinate any tendency on your part to dominate or rule. This goes against God's word as presented in our *Royal Epic*, but the rebel Job also found many things to correct in our traditions. When God says to Cain that Sin is a Demon, who desires you, he adds, 'But you will rule him.' It turns out that this may have been God's hope, but it is not the way it ended (Genesis 4:7). Earlier God says to the woman, 'Your desire is for your husband, but he will rule you.' (Genesis 3:16) This may be the orthodox position, but this is not only wrong but does not match the reality. May your equality blossom and let your passion abound."

Khety said, "What you have just said reminds me of a line from an Egyptian love song. The maiden says, 'My lover makes me the greatest of all women. He does not break my heart.' I have watched the love between Sharmila and Naam grow during several years, and I see a wonderful future for them."

I cannot remember all that was said, but I do remember that we had a great time. It was also an opportunity to get to know Samuel. We talked about the next wedding; Rachel and Samuel wanted to get married soon.

I do remember some of Abdi-anati's talk. Abdi-anati said, "I want to thank all of you for your great hospitality. This trip has been a real success, because two of your students, Joseph and Jacob, who are with us this evening, have agreed to come to Beth-shan and work as scribes. This wedding day is a great moment in our lives, but it does mean that Sharmila will not be going home with us. That brings about one of those strange mixtures; I am both glad and sad at the same time."

He was happy, but there were tears in his eyes. He wished us well, and he asked me to bring his daughter to visit whenever possible. I embraced him and promised that we would visit often.

We had plenty of wine, which inspired some singing before the rest left me to join the women's party. Alone I paced the front porch, and even though the procession would be short, it seemed to me as if they were not in a hurry to start it. But finally they did arrive, with my bride, with gifts, and with laughter. Abdi-anati brought Sharmila to me. As I lifted her veil, everyone cheered, and I kissed her before our families and friends. As I picked her up to carry her over the threshold, I said to the others, "She is the right one."

On our way to the bedroom, we noticed that Tamar had set her table with all kinds of food and drink. I stopped for a moment at the table and said, "And thank you, Tamar," but Sharmila pulled me on to the bedroom. I gladly followed. We undressed as fast as we could. I had never seen such beauty. Sharmila was gorgeous, and yes my throat was in great pain. We kissed and fell together on the bed. After much loving and even a bit of sleep, we noticed that it was dark. I said, "Do you want me to light a lamp, and we could eat something?"

"Not really," Sharmila said as she pulled me closer. "I don't want this night to ever pass."

It did pass. When it was light we got up and ate some delicious food from Tamar's table. Sharmila said that the women had a wonderful party. There were no speeches, but rather stories about Sharmila and me. Mothers seem to remember everything about their young children.

We finally went over to Sheva and Sarah's place where we found that my folks and Sheva and Sarah had remained overnight to help Sharmila's family get packed and on their way. When we entered the house, everyone hugged us and informed us that they were about to call us. Sharmila's father was anxious to get started on their long trip. Not a few tears were shed as we all said good-bye.

Mother told us that Tamar and Khety had suggested that Sharmila and I stay at their place for a few days before returning to Jerusalem. I said, "That will be wonderful, but I am also wondering what we will do when we come back to Jerusalem."

"You will stay with us," Mother said. "We will figure it out when things become too crowded."

11

WE HAD A WONDERFUL three days with fresh food and lots of loving. It would have been great to stay longer, but I did need to finish my preparations for my classes. On the first day after we returned to Jerusalem, Sharmila stayed at the house and helped Mother with her work. I went to see Khety, because I needed some help on some passages in *The Story of Sinuhe* and some answers to a few other questions.

Khety was in his office, and he greeted me with his usual smile. "You have survived the first few days of married life," he said. "I'm sure you had a great time, and I want to tell you it will even get better."

"I don't understand how it could get better, but I will take your word for it."

"So, what is on your mind this morning?"

"I need some help on a few passages in *Sinuhe*, and I have some questions that center around a project I would like to start."

"What is the project?"

"I would like to start a dictionary. Magon has said that in ancient Ugarit the scribes created a four-language dictionary with a column for each language. Ugarit was destroyed about two hundred years ago, and he has never seen a text of this dictionary. Some of the old scribes from Tyre knew a little bit about it, but they only remembered a few simple examples that others had described for them. There were four vertical columns. Starting on the left there was the Sumerian, then Babylonian, then Hurrian, and finally Ugaritic. With Magon's help, I have made a chart of a few examples they remembered:

Sumerian	Babylonian	Hurrian	Ugaritic		*Meaning*
ZA	at-ta	ši-ni-bi	at-ta	('at) =	"you"
NU	la-a	ma-nu-ku	la-a	(l) =	"no"
EN	šar-ru	i-wi-ir-ni	ma-al-ku	(mlk) =	"king"

In the Ugaritic column there is the Ugaritic pronunciation written out in Babylonian syllables instead of just the Ugaritic consonants, which is helpful, and following that I have given the Ugaritic word as it was usually written. I think we should do something like this. We don't know enough Hurrian or Ugaritic to have a column for those languages, but we could delete them and just put in Egyptian and the language of Canaan. Perhaps Magon and his students could add a Babylonian column later. We could even start with the words that are the same in Egyptian and our language, the language of Canaan. What do you think about such a project?"

"Well, I think you are on to something important. You have given it a lot of thought, and I think we should start it. Perhaps we could take a trip to Ugarit and look for their dictionary. That would be fun. For now, we will stand a better chance of getting others to help if, as you suggest, we start with a small project. We should start with the Egyptian words that are identical in the language of Canaan. This will interest others who would like to add another column to our small project. And if we ever get to your larger idea, it would be an on-going project."

"Khety, I thank you."

"We should both start a list of such words. And then we will meet to discuss our work. But you also said that you needed some help on *Sinuhe*."

"Right. I have finished most of my translation, but I do need some help on a few passages. When can I bring them and get your help?"

"I will be free in two days. Come right after lunch."

"I'll be here."

"Give my best to your lovely wife."

"Will do."

I left for home at once. I wanted to see Sharmila, and I was hungry. I also wanted to share my ideas for a new project with father. When I came through the door Sharmila ran to greet me. She gave me a nice kiss accompanied by the giggling of my dear sisters. Father was already seated at the table, and mother was putting the food on the table. We had a great meal and mother gave credit to Sharmila for her help. Father said that we would not starve with four women planning the meals.

Mother answered, "Jonathan, you would not starve if only one of the four were here. We each have our own unique contribution to make, and any one of us could keep you from starving."

"I believe you," he said. "And what did you do today, Naam?"

"I talked with Khety about making a dictionary. At Ugarit they had four language dictionaries, and I thought we could do something like that. We decided to start with the language of Canaan and Egyptian, and then perhaps others would join the effort."

Father said, "That is a great idea, and I am certain that Magon could add the Babylonian and even some Ugaritic words."

"He has already helped me some, and I showed father the chart that Magon helped me make of the Ugaritic dictionary. I will try to see him tomorrow about some additional help."

"This would be helpful; this is an important project."

" But father, what have you been doing lately?"

"I have been concerned about David and his visions of power. The evening before your wedding, just after you, Sharmila, Rachel, and Samuel went for a walk, I read a recent psalm of David. He claims to speak as God and sees his regime as having an eternal covenant with God. This is not good."

"Mother told me about that discussion. I suppose that means we have to watch for any serious developments from his new views."

"That we will, and especially when he dies and his successor takes over."

We quit talking about such things and enjoyed our meal. Sharmila and I went to the roof to spend the night. It was wonderful making love with my beautiful Sharmila under the moonlight, and we had a good rest even though we also talked for quite awhile.

Sharmila wanted to help me make some copies of *Sinuhe* and of the beginnings of the dictionary.

The next morning it did not take long to write up a few word that were the same in both the language of Canaan and Egyptian. I thought that if I did this, Magon could help with the Babylonian and Ugaritic parallels. This would go beyond our original plan, but it would be interesting to see. When I saw Magon he said, " I thought from your questions a few days ago that you would proceed with this."

He looked at my short list. He was amazing. It only took a few moments for him to add Ugaritic to most of the words, but since I was dealing mainly with words that were the same in each language, he did not always have such a word in Babylonian. So I went home and began my first draft. I wanted to be able to show it to Khety when I saw him again."

The Jerusalem Academy Dictionary				
The Languages of				
Canaan	**Egypt**	**Babylon**	**Ugarit**	*Meaning*
ʾabbîr	ibr	abaru	ʾibr	"to be strong" also "bull/stallion"
ʾozen	idn	uznu	ʾudn	"ear"
ʾanoki	ink	anaku	ʾank	"I"
zeret	drt		drt	"span"
yad	d	idu	yd	"hand"
yareaḥ	iʿḥ	warḫu	yrḥ	"moon"
leb	ib	libbu	lb	"heart/mind"
lamah	rm		lm	"why"
mut	m(w)t	matu	mt	"to die"

I had a few more examples, but I thought that this was enough to show what a dictionary would look like. Sharmila made a few copies of this. As she was working she wanted to know why some words changed a letter like "d" to "z." I explained that this sound shift was common among these languages. Also she asked about the word "why." Only in Egyptian does it have "r" instead of "l." I had to say that I did not know why, but Egyptian used the "r" to stand for both sounds. She said that this all sounded complicated. I agreed, and said, "It will take years to complete this project."

As usual Khety was happy, and he was impressed with the sample dictionary. He said that we must organize this project and expect it to go on for several years, and he said, "I will take this up at our next meeting of the faculty. Then he asked, "Did you bring your translation of *Sinuhe*?"

"Yes, I brought it, and I have a few questions."

"But first, how did you like the story?"

"I thought it was great. It is a good story, and it will help me to have an interesting class. I will compare the stories of our ancestors in *The Royal Epic* with *Sinuhe*. There are parallels not only in the content of the stories, but also in the way they tell the stories. It is clear that these prose stories, with a bit of poetry thrown in, have much in common."

"In Egypt this is one of our favorite stories. There are many copies of it, and it remains popular even though it is almost a thousand years old."

"One of my questions has to do with the Egyptian word 'ib.' Sometimes it seems to mean 'heart,' and in other places it means, 'mind.' Usually I can tell by its context what meaning to give it but not always. Of course it is both fortunate and confusing that in our language '*leb*' can also mean 'heart' or 'mind.' Perhaps I don't have to decide, but this is not really of much help to my reader."

"I think in some situations you will have to add a word that makes it clear, and in some cases we have already done that in Egyptian. I'll give you an example. Let me see your translation. Yes. Here it is in the first two lines of this poem:

My mind was blurred.
My heart, it was not in my body.

"Sinuhe is trying to explain why he left Egypt. By the way I like your translation, and you did the first two lines just right."

"But I was not certain. This is why I asked the question. In this case I felt I had to understand '*ib*' as 'mind' in the first line because in the second line of the Egyptian text another word was used for 'heart.' Then I began to think: perhaps this word pair was used in these two lines like we do in our poetry. Are they parallel in some way? But the translation is still confusing, because when I translate it into the language of Canaan, I have the same word in both lines."

"You do, but I think you got it right. A mind can be 'blurred' but not a heart. The storyteller wanted you to understand, 'mind' in the first line, and he used another word for 'heart' in the second line, which would not be misunderstood. You are learning that translation is not easy."

"Khety, it is always good for me to talk with you about such things. Things become clear in the conversation."

"Well, we all need to discuss such matters. We need each other."

"Since we have looked at this poem, I would like to ask you about it. When it appears later on in the text, it is in a different form. Here it is:

Now, this flight, which your servant made:
I did not plan it.
It was not in my heart.
I did not devise it.
I do not know what separated me from (my) place.
It was like following a dream.
(As if a man of the marshes sees himself in Elephantine,
or a man of the marsh in Nubia.)
I was not afraid.
No one had run after me.
I did not hear an abusive word.

>My name was not heard from the mouth of herald.
>But my body shivered.
>My feet were running.
>My heart moved me.
>The god who commanded this flight drew me on.

"Here in line two of the poem I went with "heart," but lines one and three contain verbs that really describe what the mind does, so, I may be wrong. Am I?"

"I think if you use your '*leb*,' which can cover both meanings, you cannot go wrong, but this is a difficult one."

"What about lines six and seven? They do not seem to fit, and I almost left them out."

"It is difficult. I have seen some texts that put these lines in the first appearance of this poem. I do not have any suggestion at this point, but I would leave it in the poem. I do like the first poem better than this second one. I notice that in both of them God gets the credit for the flight. I will need a few days to look at your entire translation, so we should meet again."

After a few more questions, we realized it was time for both of us to go home. We walked together enjoyjng the walk and the shade at that time of the day.

As soon as I got home I noticed the delicious smell of fresh bread. We had a great meal; it was good to be back around that old table but this time with my lovely new wife.

12

AFTER DINNER SHARMILA AND I washed the dishes and cleaned up the kitchen area. Ruth and Elissa helped mother put away the food. Father said, "I should be helping, but I am enjoying just watching the rest of you. Also I seem to be tired tonight."

"You need to get more rest," mother said. "I hope that you can put David's claims to greater powers out of your mind for now. We need a change of pace. I would like to take a trip down to Ziklag and visit my mother's grave. We have not been there for some time and the trip would be good for us. Naam and Sharmila could look after the girls."

Father answered, "You're so right. I need to get away. I not only worry about David and who will succeed him, but many who detest my rebel Job are still pestering me. I think we should leave tomorrow."

Sharmila and I both agreed with the plan, but mother said, "I will need tomorrow to get ready. We can leave the next day."

"That's fine," Father said. "I could use the extra day to get ready as well."

They left on their trip, and the girls spent most of their time with friends. Sharmila and I had lots of time for loving, walking, and working. I was still trying to get ready for my classes, and she was catching up on a journal she had started. Her journal has been important for the writing of this story.

I had to re-read the stories of our ancestors in *The Royal Epic*, and I was still working on my translation of some Egyptian stories. It slowly dawned on me that most of the detailed similarities in the two groups of prose narratives were found in *The Story of Joseph* and *The Story of Sinuhe*. For the first day of my class, I decided to make a list of the more general structural parallels. I listed five of these.

First, the stories of *The Shipwrecked Sailor*, *The Enchanted Prince*, *The Story of Sinuhe, and The Journey of Wenamon* are written in prose though there is some poetry in *The Story of Sinuhe*. In the stories of Abraham, Isaac, Jacob, and Joseph, we also have prose stories with some poetry. I should add that when our *Royal Epic* was produced most of the stories about Isaac were not used. This omission was discussed in mother's *The Jerusalem Academy;* only the stories of Rebekah's journey to Canaan and Isaac and Rebekah's stay in Gerar are included (Genesis 24 and 26). Egypt and Israel have used prose for such stories, and their neighbors have used poetry. In my opinion the prose stories have given us a greater audience. People feel close to their heroes in these stories. Poetry may have great insights and is a means to elevate feelings and events, but our people want to be entertained and brought together in the language that surrounds their lives.

Second, in these stories the hero always goes on a long journey. The journeys are undertaken for various reasons: a royal mission, the search for food during times of famine, or fears that lead to exile. Most of the people in the audience have never been able to travel for any reason, and these travels create and surround them with adventure. They like these stories.

Third, travel and adventure expose the hero to danger, and in these stories danger is always present. The dangers range from shipwrecks to threats by kings, warriors, relatives, and divinities.

Fourth, the hero is able to have great success in spite of the dangers. He is brave and powerful. Sometimes his wife helps him, and always he obtains an abundance of riches, either by the result of his work or as outright gifts.

Fifth, in each story there is an emphasis on the return or the home-coming. This is an important event always followed by a great celebration. One purpose of the return is to bury the hero in his homeland. In our own stories the return is not always before the death of the hero, but even so the hero is returned and buried in his own land.

On the first day of class, I also gave a copy of my new translation of *Sinuhe* to each student. As I stood before them, I gave them the following summary:

"The story opens with a scribe introducing the reader to Sinuhe. This scribe seems to follow a typical pattern of a titulary for kings, which in a formal document would give the five names of the king. Likewise, Sinuhe is given five titles: prince, ruler, administrator, friend of the king, and orderly. It is interesting that later on in the story Sinuhe gives the five names of the Egyptian king, Sesostris. After this we have Sinuhe's first person account. We are informed that Pharaoh (Amenemhet I) has been killed. Sinuhe never makes it clear why he is fearful in this situation, but he does say that he is afraid there will be a civil war. So he flees Egypt and goes into exile.

"He goes north spending some time in Byblos and Qedem. Finally he arrives in northern Syria. He stays with Ammi-enshi, the ruler of

Upper Retenu, who asks, 'Why have you come here?' Then Sinuhe recites one of his poems:

> My mind was blurred.
> My heart, it was not in my body.
> It carried me off on the way of flight.
> No one gossiped about me.
> No one spat in my face.
> No reproach was heard.
> My name was not heard from the mouth of a herald.
> I do not know what brought me to this country.
> It was as if planned by a god.

"When asked about the new Pharaoh of Egypt, Sinuhe answers with another long poem, which extols the greatness of Sesostris. Then Sinuhe tells us about his life with Ammi-enshi:

> He placed me at the head of his children. He married me to his eldest daughter. He allowed me to choose for myself from his country, from the choicest of that which was his, on the border with another country. This land was beautiful; its name was Yaa. There were figs in it and vineyards. It had more wine than water. Its honey was abundant and plentiful its olive oil. Every kind of fruit was on its trees. There was barley along with emmer. All the cattle herds were without number. Moreover, great gifts were brought to me; they came because of the love of me. He made me chief of a tribe from the best part of his country. Bread was served to me daily (plus) a fine wine, cooked meat, roast foul, besides the wild beasts of the dessert. For they used to snare for me and would bring it for me, in addition to what my hounds caught. They made many things for me, and all were boiled in milk.

"Sinuhe says that he was the one who entertained travelers from Egypt and elsewhere, and he was also appointed as commander of the army. But then there was a great hero from Retenu who challenged Sinuhe. He wanted to fight and to take all of Sinuhe's riches. The battle scene is worth quoting:

> He came to me; I was waiting, having placed myself near him. Every heart burned for me; women and men murmured. Every heart was sick for me. They said, "Is there another hero who could fight against him?" Then he raised his shield and his axe; his armful of javelins were hurled toward me. I caused his weapons to pass by me. His arrows amounted to nothing, one after the other. Then he charged me, and I shot him. My arrow stuck in his neck. He cried

out; he fell on his face. I slew him with his axe, and I raised my war cry over his back. Every Asiatic shouted, and I gave praise to Montu.

"Though successful Sinuhe begins to think about his home land. He wants to go back. He says that his body should be buried in the land of his birth. Pharaoh hears about his longings and sends a decree telling Sinuhe to return to Egypt. Sinuhe answers the decree and agrees to return. He hands over all his property to his children, and puts his eldest son in charge of his tribe.

"When he returns to Egypt, he is presented to Pharaoh. Then he is given a home; he is cleaned up; his hair is combed; he is dressed in fine linen; he is anointed with oil; he passes the night in a bed; and his clothing and the sand is returned to the those who dwell on the sand. They also build for him a tomb. Finally he says, 'I was under the favor of the king until the coming day of mooring.'"

After this summary, the entire class wanted to read the complete story, and I told them to come up with parallels to our own stories in *The Royal Epic*.

13

I WALKED HOME AND was greeted by my sisters and Sharmila. "Did my girls have an interesting day?"

Before they could answer, there was a knock on the door. I went to the door, and Benaiah ben Jehoiada, commander of the Cherethites and the Pelethites, was standing there with message in hand. He asked, "Is Jonathan here?"

"No he is not. He has gone with my mother to Ziklag to visit the grave of my grandmother. May I help you?"

He handed the message to me, saying, "You can give him this message as soon as he returns. King David wants to see him. The king is not pleased that your father has not responded to an earlier message that contained the king's poem dealing with his *Last Words*."

"I'll see that he gets this."

With that Benaiah joined his guards and left.

Sharmila asked me, "Who was that?"

"That was Benaiah. He is the commander of David's personal guard, made up of mercenaries from Crete and other western islands usually referred to as the Cherethites and the Pelethites. They were also mercenaries for the Egyptians in Beth-Shan, your hometown. It is interesting that not far from Beth-Shan there is the Wady Krit (or Crete), which may refer in some way to these mercenaries. They left Beth-Shan when David arrived and joined with their brothers, the Philistines. I take it that they will fight for anyone who pays. Perhaps some of them did not join with the Philistines but rather with David."

"Benaiah was certainly all business."

Ruth said, "He's a scary man."

"And a powerful man. Even so, father will not be pleased with this or with David's displeasure."

When father and mother arrived home the next day, I asked about their trip. Apparently it was not an easy trip, and the conditions in Ziklag were awful. But they spent some time at grandmother's grave and telling again her story. I gave father the message from David. He read it and tore it up. He said, "David's *Last Words* are so awful that I hope they are his last words. It may not be wise, but I intend to make him wait for my opinion. He is getting old, out of touch, and forgetful, but we do have to worry about his successor's attitude concerning David's *Last Words*."

That evening Sharmila said to me, "Rachel was here today. She and Samuel are getting married in a few weeks, but it will all take place at Shechem. Samuel is from there as well as Rachel's folks. Of course you knew that. But I don't think we should try to go to Shechem."

"Why not?"

"Because, as I told Rachel, I am carrying our first child."

I could not believe it. I gently embraced her and kissed her, and I said, "This is wonderful."

"I think so as well, but I would rather have a strong hug. I won't break."

We immediately told the rest of the family, and as anyone could guess, mother already knew about the good news.

The next morning we were eating and I said to father, "This morning I have my second class-session on *The Stories of Our Ancestors* and *The Story of Sinuhe*. One parallel that will be discussed is Sinuhe's battle with the hero of Retenu and David's killing of Goliath. Both are told with similar words and phrases. Do you think I should mention that there is another tradition that would question David's role in this?"

"I would mention it but don't mention the fact that Elhanan did it. They will find that out someday."

"I won't mention his name. I just want to show that a storyteller will employ, from common knowledge, some of the same details in similar stories, and these two scenes are very much alike."

"I would like to see what you do with this. Write it up for me."

"I'll do that."

Before leaving for class, I gave Sharmila a real hug.

When I reached the class building, Elyahba' stepped out from the doorway and blocked my way. Elyahba' was the priest who debated father some years ago. He hated father's poem about the rebel Job. He said, "I have heard that you are comparing the stories of our fathers with some Egyptian stories and apparently you think the Egyptian storytellers influenced our storytellers. You are wrong just like your father was wrong. David may not punish you for teaching such things, but when Adonijah becomes king, he will deal with you."

"I don't have time to deal with you now, but just come to my class and perhaps your little mind will be able to understand that you know nothing about this subject."

"I have warned you. I am making a list for Adonijah, and you are on it."

"Great. Perhaps I will ask Adonijah, at the proper time, why priests like you insist on being ignorant."

He uttered a few choice curses and left. Some of the students were amused, but one or two looked disappointed. I supposed they were the ones who had been complaining to Elyahba'. I know that irrational fundamentalists will always be around. They try to close the minds of students all in the name of loyalty to altar and to state.

I was still angry when the class started, and I told my students, "Some of you overheard my argument with Elyahba' a few moments ago. Someone or a few of you apparently complained to him, or perhaps he asked you about the class and you informed him. In the future if you have questions or doubts about any of this material, come and see me. We will be able to discuss it in detail.

"Today I assume that you have read *Sinuhe*, and I want to go over some of the parallels. You may add to the discussion at any time. It seems that the scribe, who introduces Sinuhe to the reader, sees him as a ruler in a foreign land. He is certainly a ruler of Egyptian holdings and perhaps of entire lands and their peoples. There is no doubt that he ruled in Yaa. Here he was made commander of the army of Retenu, and he ruled his own tribe. We can say similar things about Joseph. He did not displace Pharaoh, but he had great power. As we continue along these lines, we will see many parallels in the way in which Joseph was treated and the way in which Sinuhe was honored.

"At our last meeting, I mentioned some of the following points. These stories always start in a time of danger for the hero. In Sinuhe's case, a new king was about to take over. This is interesting in the light of Elyahba's comments this morning. He threatened me concerning a future event: namely, the rule of Adonijah after the death of David. He thought a new king would know what to do with me. Perhaps I should run, but I think not. Now back to our stories. When Jacob left on his trip to the north, he left under the threats of Esau. Joseph was in grave danger from his brothers when he was taken to Egypt. This always makes an interesting beginning. But the hero is always able to overcome obstacles and becomes successful and rich in material goods.

"Some of the parallels are about the words and phrases that were used to express similar situations. 'Jacob directed his feet to the Land of the Bene-qedem (or 'lifted his feet,' Gen 29:1).' Sinuhe says, 'I set (*rdit.i*) my feet on the road going north.' It is interesting that Sinuhe also went to Qedem.

"In these stories there is an interest in finding out where the travelers are from and how they got to the present place. In *The Story of the Shipwrecked Sailor,* the serpent asks, 'Who brought you to this island?' In *The Enchanted Prince* the other princes ask, 'Where do you come from?' In our stories the question is often answered before it is asked. This is the case with Jacob. Sinuhe says, 'I do not know what brought me to this country. It was as if planned by a god.' Again I am reminded of what Joseph said to his brothers, 'Elohim sent me ahead of you' (Genesis 45:5).

"When Sinuhe is given the eldest daughter of Ammi-anshi, it tells us a lot about Jacob and Leah (Genesis 29:26). At least it shows that it was an ancient tradition. Jacob should have known that he would get Leah rather than Rachel.

"I am at this point not putting these things in any order. I am just bringing them up as I think through the story. There are some things in *Sinuhe* that parallel our own traditions. Note his proverb. 'Is a poor man loved when he is appointed as a ruler over me?' In our proverbs there is a section about what will cause the earth to shudder. One item is expressed this way: 'A slave who becomes king'" (Proverbs 30:22a).

One of my students said, "In your summary at our last class meeting and when I was reading *Sinuhe*, I was astounded by the part concerning his fight with a hero of Retenu. It sounded very much like the stories that I have heard about David's defeat of Goliath."

"These stories use the same storyteller's art. The Egyptians have taught us all how to tell good stories. Actually we have at least two traditions about the killing of Goliath, but the one that will never be changed gives the credit to David. It is a lot like the *Sinuhe* account that you have just read."

Another student asked, "Why do you say that it will never be changed?"

"Because the administration's story about any event cannot be changed. New evidence that could change a story is just not allowed or taken seriously."

"So, what can be done?"

"The only thing one can do is to keep all of the traditions alive and well, and as my mother has pointed out in her book, *The Minority Report*, the minority opinions can be the most essential for our future.

"It may be important to note that the age of our ancestors is coming to a close. The stories of our ancestors were recited at their tombs, and these stories give us the background that points the way to David, and in like manner the stories of David that will be recited at his tomb will certainly include his killing of Goliath, told in the same way as this tale concerning Sinuhe was told at his tomb. I think we should read both accounts again. First let's read the *Sinuhe* account:

> Then came a hero of Retenu,
> To challenge me in my own camp.
> He was a champion, this one, without equal.
> He had subdued all of it.
> He said he would fight with me.
> He intended to rob me.
> He planned to take my cattle,
> On the counsel of his tribe.
>
> . . .

> He came to me; I was waiting, having placed myself near him. Every heart burned for me; women and men murmured. Every heart was sick for me. They said, "Is there another hero who could fight against him? Then he raised his shield and his axe; his armful of javelins were hurled toward me. I caused his weapons to pass by me. His arrows amounted to nothing, one after the other. Then he charged me, and I shot him. My arrow stuck in his neck. He cried out; *he fell on his face*. I slew him with *his* axe, and I raised my war cry over his back. Every Asiatic shouted, and I gave praise to Montu.

"Now here is the popular tradition of the killing of Goliath:

> So it happened that the Philistine came and drew near in order to meet David. David hurried; he ran to the battle line to meet the Philistine. David put his hand into the bag; he took from it a stone. He slung it. He hit the Philistine's brow; the stone penetrated into it. *He fell on his face to the ground.* David prevailed over the Philistine with the sling and with the stone. He hit the Philistine; he killed him, and there was not a sword in the hand of David.

> David ran.
> He stood on the Philistine.

He took *his* sword;
He drew it from its sheath.
He killed him.
He cut off his head with it. (1 Samuel 17:48–51a)

"These accounts are told in a delightful manner, true or not." Then I asked, "What are the similarities in these two accounts?"

No one was offering any answer to the question, so I said, "There are several interesting parallels in these stories, but two are outstanding. In both, the enemy falls on his face. In Akkadian letters, the inferior person begins with obeisance or homage to the addressee. The ruler of Jerusalem, 'Abdi-Heba, says in a letter that he sent to Egypt about three-hundred years ago, 'I fall at the feet of my lord, the king [in this case Pharaoh], 7 times and 7 times.' By falling on his face the opponent becomes a 'servant' to Sinuhe or to David, albeit in these cases dead servants. Also we note that in both stories the hero uses the opponent's weapon to kill him and in David's case to cut off his head."

I offered one more example: "You will note that Sinuhe is prepared for his new life by being bathed. His hair is combed, and he is dressed in fine linen. When Joseph was brought out of prison or the pit he was prepared to meet the Pharaoh. 'He shaved; he changed his clothes,' (Genesis 41:14) and Pharaoh 'dressed him in linen' (Genesis 41:42). When we point out such parallels, we are not saying anything about the truth of the story. It has to do with what you say and what you don't say. A good storyteller knows that it is important to mention 'fine linen.'

"There are many more things that you will notice if you read the story with care. At our next meeting, we will discuss the story of Wen-Amon. I put two copies of my translation in the library."

After class several students asked me questions. Some of the questions were thoughtful, but the students who did not like what we were doing hurried out of the room.

14

IT WAS GETTING LATE, so I hurried home. I was hungry, and I was anxious to tell the rest of the family about Elyahba'. When I got there everyone had just sat down at the table. Walking around the table, I gave Sharmila a kiss and mother as well. Elissa and Ruth refused such greetings but not my dear father. Mother said, "You seem happy."

"I am happy. My class went well."

Then I told them about Elyahba' and his threats. "He seemed to be certain that Adonijah would be the next king, and Adonijah would know what to do with the likes of us."

"Adonijah has the backing of Joab, who is back in Jerusalem, and of Abiathar, the priest, but I doubt he will ever be king," father answered. "Solomon has a much better chance."

"Well, I hope you are right."

About half way through our meal mother said, " I have some sad news, and some good news. Jonathan, you have known that this was coming for some time, but it will be new to the rest of you. Sheva has not been feeling well. He wants your father to take over the leadership of the academy. Sarah said that they want to move out to their estate. Also they have suggested that our fine son and his beautiful wife should live in their house."

Sharmila was obviously excited, and she said, "I am sorry to hear that Sheva is ill. Do you think he will get better in the country?"

"I'm sure that he will," father answered.

"It is a wonderful thing for us that they want us to move to their house," Sharmila continued. "Will this happen before the baby comes?"

Father answered, "I would think so. I have been dragging my feet on this, because I never wanted an administrative job. I tried to talk El-ishama, Rachel's father, into this job, but he is still too busy with Part II of our *Royal Epic*. But Sheva is really not well, and I will take over but perhaps for just a limited time. The answer, Sharmila, is yes; it will be soon. Sheva must get some rest now."

" We should help Sarah and Sheva with their moving," I said.

"We will do that," said mother.

After we helped to move Sarah and Sheva, we moved into their house. Father took Sheva's job, and David sent some orders about what he wanted done. Father was overjoyed that David did not mention his *Last Words* again. David wanted father to start a project of collecting all our psalms, and father asked Samuel to work with Hanani, the son of Heman, on this. Heman had been one of our greatest minstrels for years, and Hanani was the minstrel who had helped father on several occasions. These two could get this project started.

Another thing that David wanted father to do was to make sure all his words and acts were recorded in his chronicle. Father soon found out that he had three documents to deal with: one by Samuel for David's early years, another by Nathan, David's current prophet, from the middle years to the present, and a third by Gad, my mother's father, for the middle years. He decided that he would have to do some catch up work and then keep it up to date until David's death. Also, he had another problem in that Nathan and my grandfather disagreed on many things in their works. My grandfather was never just a yes-man. Father decided to just let the disagreements stand side-by-side. However, somehow Nathan heard about father's decision and was angry.

One evening as father entered his office, he was hit on the head from behind. He fell down. As he was falling he grabbed the intruder's leg, who was attempting to escape. The intruder kicked free and ran out. Though he was still on the floor, father saw that he had a scroll in his left hand. When father got up and looked around, he soon discovered that Gad's chronicles were gone.

The next morning father went to see David to complain about the robbery. David summoned Nathan. When Nathan arrived, he denied that he was involved in any way, but then he said that he was glad that someone took Gad's work. He said that Gad was a critic not a prophet. Then David said to father, "We will try to find out what happened, but it will be difficult."

"You asked me to work on the chronicles, and now I am missing one scroll. You had your troubles with Gad, and Nathan was always jealous of Gad. That does not mean that Gad's work was of no use. I don't know how Nathan found out about my work on these documents, but he did. You heard him. Now he is glad. As far as I am concerned, his mouth has condemned him. Besides, you already know what I think about Nathan for what he and Hushai did to my Job poem or *Job II*; they buried it in the ancient story of Job. David we grew up together. We have had our differences, but your prophet has no business interfering with our work in the academy. Also I seem to remember a commandment: 'You shall not steal.'"

Since father was David's uncle (but ten years younger), he could get away with talking to him like that, but that does not mean that David would do anything about it. One thing that father did know was that his head was still aching from the blow he had received.

At lunch that day father received a surprise. As he sat down at the table, he noticed a scroll at his place. He opened it, and he could not believe the opening line: *sepher divrey gad*, "the book of the chronicles of Gad." His first words were, "Where did this come from?"

Mother's answer was short, "From the crypt."

We had a cellar where mother hid scrolls in jars. There she kept copies of her work, of father's *Job II*, and of grandfather's work. She explained to father and the rest of us, "When you left this morning to see David, I could not remember if I had a copy of father's work on David in one of my jars. After you left, I looked and I found this one."

Father got up; he walked around the table; he kissed mother, and he said, "You are a wonderful woman. My head even feels better."

Sharmila said, "I will make a copy, and then you can keep one here and take one to the office."

Father said, "Thank you. That is a great plan."

"This is such an interesting and important project," I said. "Also it is helpful for me, because tomorrow I will be discussing with my class how, in the Egyptian report by Wen-Amon, Zakar-Ba'al, the Prince of Byblos, wants to check what happened in the past. In order to do this, he calls for his ancestors' *Scrolls of the Days*. Father, this is just like the important documents you are trying your best to preserve. These we also call *sefer divrey hayyamim (The scroll of the words/acts of the days).*"

"Naam, you have allowed me to see how important this can be. All the states in our world have kept such records for many years, and they will be helpful in the future if we can keep all of them and not re-write our past. To re-write simplifies the events, but it usually crowds out the many voices—especially the minority voices. I am so glad to have in my hand the chronicles of Gad. Thanks you Keziah."

15

WE DECIDED THAT WE were going to be careful from now on and would keep things in a safe place. We were on edge for a few days. By the time things were better, it was time for my class dealing with Wen-Amon.

Khety and I never did obtain a better copy of Wen-Amon, and that means we do not have the ending of the report. But as Khety remembers the story, Wen–Amon did get back to Egypt and was able to write this report. I reminded the class that this report was written about a hundred years ago. It does not have as many literary parallels to our stories as *The Story of Sinuhe*, but there are matters of vocabulary, descriptions of life and work along the coast, and political activities that we should know. Magon, who is from Tyre, sees it as presenting an excellent picture of the times.

The first thing that I discussed was the meaning of the name Wen-Amon. I think the meaning is obvious. What is interesting to anyone who also works with the languages of Canaan, Tyre, Ugarit, and Babylon is that the pattern is typical. The first element (*Wen* in this case) means "there is/ are" or "to exist," and the second element is of course a divine name. So we have the meaning, "Amon exists/lives," and this is helpful when dealing with examples from our neighbors, which follow this pattern: 1) From Tyre we have, *'ithba'al*, 2) from the language of Canaan, *'eshba'al*, 3) from Ugarit, *'ishba'al* (related to the phrase, *'ithba'al*, "Ba'al lives"), 4) Babylonian, *'i-shi-ba'al*. The first element in all of these means, "to exist," and the second element is, of course, the god Ba'al. Many of our scribes have made the mistake of seeing the first element as meaning, "man." This mistake can be seen in the way some have changed the name of Saul's son, *'eshba'al*, meaning, "Ba'al lives," to *'ishbosheth*, "Man of shame." This point is not a great discovery, but it is a reminder that we can achieve a better understanding of our own language by these studies.

Next, I told the students that there were words in *The Story of Wen-Amon* that they would know, because they are the same in our language, for example, *yamm*, "sea" and the verb, *m(w)t*, "to die." Also there are grammatical formations that are the same. There are even similar idioms, for example, "Then he answered and said to me." And then I said, "One interesting part for me is when Zakar-Baʿal, the Prince of Byblos, wants to prove a point to Wen-Amon. In order to do this, he sends for the records. The text says, 'Then he ordered his ancestors' *Scrolls of the Days.*' This is almost the same way we refer to our chronicles: *sefer divrey hayyamim* (*The scroll of the words/acts of the days*). I am interested in the fact that they kept written records in the same way that we keep written records. In fact, just now David has asked Jonathan, my father, who has now been put in charge of our academy, to prepare his chronicles. We have many oral traditions, but the keeping of chronicles has been with us for many years."

Then I told my class that I was interested in Zakar-Baʿal's statement about the importance of Egypt. Here is how he put it:

> Indeed, Amon has established all the lands. When he established them, he established first the Land of Egypt from which you have come. Thus craftsmanship came from it to reach the place where I am, and wisdom came from it to reach the place where I am.

The first part of this is like the old tradition that we have in *The Song of Moses*:

> When Elyon allotted states an inheritance,
> When he divided up humanity,
> He established boundaries of peoples,
> According to the number of the sons of God.
> For Yahweh's portion is his people,
> Jacob his allotted inheritance." (Deuteronomy 32:8–9)

Then I said, "Some of our people do not like this old tradition, because Yahweh appears as one of the 'sons of God' and Elyon is the head of the pantheon. In fact Elyon functions, as does Amon, in 'establishing all the lands.' Also, it may be even more important for us to note that the Prince of Byblos gives credit to Egypt for its gift of 'craftsmanship' and 'wisdom' whereas priests like Elyahba' think we should not give so much credit to the Egyptian storytellers."

At this point one student said, "This is interesting, but if Wen-Amon wrote this, or even some other Egyptians, couldn't he have exaggerated the grateful response of the Prince for the gift of wisdom from Egypt?"

"Yes, and we should always ask these kinds of questions. But in this case I don't think Wen-Amon would try in any way to make the Prince look better. The report was written after his return to Egypt, and the Prince was not really helpful. Certainly, the Prince did not deserve any favors from Wen-Amon. He placed Wen-Amon in a dangerous situation in order to get rid of him."

Finally, I wanted to emphasize some things that were not great moments, but they were interesting observations. Once when Wen-Amon was going to see the Prince he said, "I found him (in) his upper room, leaning his back against a window, and the waves of the great sea of Syria were breaking behind his head."

I told my class that in our writing we should take time to describe or set the scene, and I said, "This is really a beautiful portrait of the Prince sitting before the window with the breakers of the sea in the background. It is a wonderful picture. I think we should be more interested in the beauty of our surroundings."

There are other observations that make this story so real. Wen-Amon is weeping, because he has been on this trip for such along time. A scribe asked him, "What's with you?"

Wen-Amon said to him, "Haven't you seen the migrating birds go down to Egypt two times? Look at them! They are traveling from the cool water."

I said to the class, "I think most of us know something about migrating birds, but somehow we don't take the time to include such comments in our writings.

"I have told you that the ending of this report is lost from our text. But Khety has told me that he remembers that Wen-Amon did finally get home. We do not know when he got home. Perhaps it took him a long time, because he was at sea, and the wind drove him to Alashiya (Cyprus). As you know, he was in grave danger, but he called on Hatiba, the Princess, to help him. She not only helped him, but the last words of our text are from her. She said to Wen-Amon, 'Spend the night.' Since the Egyptians were good storytellers, it is not difficult to imagine that the Princess was beautiful and that We-Amon stayed for several nights."

It was time to finish, and so we left without the usual questions and answers.

16

Sharmila and I were moved into our new home, but as yet we were not settled, and we still had our evening meals with my family. So after class, I came home, and then we walked over there for dinner.

Father was interested in my treatment of Wen-Amon. I explained to him before dinner what I had said about the words of the Prince of Byblos concerning the gifts of Egypt. He said, "This is an important observation. Many of us do not think about it, but we are indebted to the Prince of Byblos and others from Tyre for so many things. We got our alphabet from them, which was a tremendous gift; we will always be dependent upon them for their knowledge of the sea and shipping; we used their knowledge and skill in the building of David's palace; and we cannot forget the contributions of our friend and colleague, Magon of Tyre. Their attitude concerning Egypt's gifts of craftsmanship and wisdom is why they have so much to give. If we want to make things better for future generations, we must remain open and willing to receive help from our friends in this world of ours, who have enjoyed many years of experience before we existed as a people."

"It is so helpful to be able to talk about such things," I said. "I was so taken with the gifts of Egypt that I had not thought about what others had given to us. In fact, it is interesting to me how we come up with some of our observations. I had only intended to compare how Amon had established all the lands with the similar claim in our traditions that Elyon had done the same. But within the dynamics of the class session, I found myself talking about these gifts from Egypt."

At this point, mother called us to the table. As usual, we went to the table for our favorite time of day. Mother said to me, "As I was finishing the meal preparations, I was listening to you, and I know the feeling. In the midst of a conversation, I suddenly get a new idea, or I start writing, and I take off in an unplanned direction."

Sharmila added, "Sometimes I cannot think of how to continue a poem, but if I just start writing something happens. Under pressure, I begin to think. In your case today, it is also possible that Elyahba' was still lurking in the depths of your mind, and suddenly you saw a perfect response to him."

"You are probably right," I said.

"I have also experienced such things," said father. "Usually such flashes of insight turn out to be important, but I always take some time and check them out. Sometimes they fail the test upon closer inspection, and at other times I can expand them."

Mother said, "I have gone to sleep thinking about a problem, and I solved it in a dream. However, the next morning in the light of day my solution made no sense at all."

I said, "Apparently we have all had some experiences like I had today. It seems that we need to be under some pressure, and if so, our minds will process the past or some story of the past and come up with a new idea that just may help us to create a better future. With my students, I am going to stress being open to past gifts and hopeful for a new future. But I know that things move at a slow pace."

Father said, "They have for us, and at times they have even moved in the wrong direction, but we can be certain of one thing: things will change."

17

As father said, "Things will change." Sharmila and I had moved into our wonderful house; we were expecting our first child; and my classes were becoming more interesting. But the larger changes in our lives were just beginning: David was getting old; he was now about seventy years old, and my father was almost sixty. The gossip was that David's health was slipping. He always seemed to be cold. His servants told him that he should look in all of Israel to find a beautiful young woman—one who could wait on him, service him, lie in his bosom, and bring him heat. After a thorough search they found the young beauty, Abishag the Shunammite. Not only were her face and figure beyond compare, but also her personality was pleasing. She had a wonderful smile and did everything possible to make David feel alive again. Even so, and judging from his continued decline, he apparently was not able to act on his desire for her. This failure brought him to a new low. One servant told father that Abishag would enter the king's chamber with high hopes but would soon leave in tears.

This gossip, be it true or false, did not help David's situation. It only fanned the flames of Adonijah's boast, "I will be king." Technically speaking, he was the next in line, and Joab and Abiathar backed him. Adonijah was good looking and had many followers. The special crowds at his so-called coronation, which was not made known to David, shouted, "Long Live King Adonijah."

Since David had promised Bathsheba that her son, Solomon, would be the next king, Adonijah should never have taken matters into his own hands. He probably followed Joab's advice, which means Adonijah was not aware of the fact that Joab did not care about him but had some other plan in mind. David may not have been well, but he did act. At least that is what the prophet Nathan, the priest Zadok, and Benaiah, commander of the Cherethites and the Pelethites, said. In any case they anointed Solomon king at the Gihon spring.

This coronation was all done in haste. There was no elaborate coronation for Solomon as there was for David at Hebron. David was still alive, and thus they could not have a coronation at his tomb. But they knew that David would be buried at this cultic center near the Gihon, and so this was the beginning of a new tradition: a place for the burial and coronation of future kings.

David died, and he was buried in his city. The tomb ritual at the Gihon was rather simple. Most of David's family, friends, officials, and guards were present. There were several minstrels to sing some of his psalms and recall the great events of his life. There were many people as well, but it was difficult for them to get close enough to hear much in the small area of the Gihon. Solomon participated in some of the ritual moments. He began by calling forth David's name:

> We call forth your name, "David."
> Hence, we call forth your person to bless us.
> You have fulfilled many roles to our benefit;
> You have been father, warrior, shepherd, and king.
> You have united Judah and Israel and made us great.
> Your enemies have said, "When will he die and his name perish?"
> But your name will never perish; your enemies will perish.
> We call forth your name and recall your story.
> We seek your blessing.

The minstrels began their songs. Some of the songs brought back great memories. David had presented us with many problems over the years, but on this occasion, we remembered him as a great person. I even saw a tear in my father's eye. No doubt he was remembering the good moments when good options were still possible. In later years my father, who could speak with David with candor, disagreed with him most of the time, but beyond their problems, David's person always remained a tremendous force. He was special.

The minstrels included the story of David and Goliath, which I had predicted in my class session. As I told my students, "It may not be factual, but David is our epic hero. The story will be told at his tomb as Sinuhe's story was told at his tomb in Egypt."

After hearing David's story, the crowd cheered, and Nathan gave the final blessing:

> Shalom!
> Shalom to Bathsheba!

Shalom to Solomon!
Shalom to the House of David!
Shalom to Jerusalem!
Shalom to her Gates!
Shalom!

Later on the day of the funeral, Nathan forwarded information to father for inclusion in David's chronicle. It was interesting. It claimed that David had given Solomon some instructions as how to deal with his internal enemies. These enemies included Adonijah, Abiathar, and Joab. This, true or not, gave Solomon just what he needed to clean house, and these "enemies" played right into his hands.

Remember that Adonijah had planned his own coronation and claim to kingship with Joab and Abiathar, the priest. It was a plot, but it failed, and Solomon was declared the new king. So, these three planned another plot. It was not an original but rather a traditional plot and one of Joab's favorite schemes. It was based on an old belief that if you sleep with one of the king's concubines, the kingdom is yours. Joab must have convinced Adonijah that doing such a thing would give him a second chance. So Adonijah approached Bathsheba and asked a favor, sayong, "Please ask King Solomon to give me the beautiful Abishag as a wife."

When Bathsheba relayed this request to Solomon, he said, "Why do you request Abishag for Adonijah? Request for him the kingdom! Your grandfather, Ahban, used this approach during the rebellion against David. He advised Absalom to have intercourse with his father's concubines (1 Samuel 16:20). This is a symbolic action that sends a message: the perpetrator takes the place of the king. Also Îshbosheth, the son of Saul, accused Abner of this approach, because Abner took Rizpah, one of Saul's concubines (2 Samuel 3:7). This cannot be allowed. For this request Adonijah will surely die."

Solomon ordered Benaiah to kill Adonijah. When Abiathar and Joab heard this news, they were frightened. Solomon exiled Abiathar to his estate at Anathoth, but Joab was not so lucky. Joab ran to the altar in the tent of Yahweh. There he grabbed the horns of the altar and said, "You will have to kill me here." Benaiah reported this to Solomon, and Solomon told Benaiah to fulfill Joab's request. Joab was buried in the wilderness.

Many people welcomed Joab death. He had killed Abner, Absalom, Amasa, my grandfather Gad, and Ahban, whom the officials now call Ahithophel. Joab tried to rape my mother, and he was vile to Tamar. After he tried to rape mother and then killed her father, my father caught him in the palace and castrated him. Even though he was one of David's sons—a fact known to only a few—he even threatened David at times. I wonder if his mother, Zeruiah, mourned his death.

18

As we gathered around the table that evening, we were not mourning the death of Joab, but we were not celebrating either. Father put it well, "This family as well as the House of David have suffered from the many evil acts of Joab. I cannot mourn his death, but there is nothing in this situation to give me hope. Our enemy is gone, but our new ruler is too efficient. I think we must be careful with Solomon as our king. I will not be able to speak frankly with him as I did with David."

"Careful we will be," I said. "Perhaps time will tell how we can continue our work and live with our new king. I have been wondering what Elyahba' is doing with his list of subversive teachers that he was making for Adonijah? His superior has been sent away, and Adonijah is dead."

Mother said, "I imagine that Elyahba' will not be bothering you for some time. In fact your Egyptian stories may be a popular subject during the coming weeks. Speaking of Egypt, I have invited Tamar and Khety to come over after their evening meal for raisin cakes and wine. Khety wants to tell us about some work that he has been doing for Solomon."

"That will be interesting," I said.

Sharmila got up from the table and said, "Naam, help me get this food put away. We can help get ready for guests, and I am anxious to hear about what Khety is doing."

When Khety and Tamar arrived we were ready, but Khety first words were not about his work with Solomon. He said, "I want Naam and Sharmila to know that we may be a bit slow, but Tamar and I are also expecting our first child."

Of course mother already knew about this. We all were happy about this news, and Tamar said, "I may be a little too old for a first child, but at least, I am not as old as Sarah was when Isaac was born. Still, if we have a boy, we probably should name him Isaac; we do need 'laughter' in our lives. If we have a girl . . . "

Khety finished this for Tamar, "If we have a girl, we will name her, Nefertiti; we also need 'beauty' in our lives. Nefertiti was not only beautiful, but she also stressed the rights of women."

Father said, "This is great news. Come to the table, and we will pour some wine."

As always we had a great time around the table. Elissa and Ruth joined in on the conversation as well. They were willing and ready to welcome not just one but two babies into our group. Plus they were both in love with 'Uncle' Khety. Finally, Mother asked Khety saying, "We would like to hear about what you have been doing for Solomon, if you can tell us."

"I can tell you, because I know that what I say will not leave this room. But perhaps we should have Magon and Naomi come over to hear this as well?"

Mother sent Elissa and Ruth across the road to ask them to come on over. Soon they were around the table, and mother said, "Khety was just about to tell us some news, and he wanted you to hear it as well."

With that, Khety continued. "The last few weeks have been interesting. As some of you know, one of the reasons I left Egypt was that the rulers, as I saw them, were not true Pharaohs but rather powerful priests from Thebes and Libyan merchants from Tanis. As we know from reading Wen-Amon, Egypt was already weak at the beginning of this period. Even though Wen-Amon was loyal to Ne-su-Ba-neb-Ded (Smendes) and his wife Tanet-Amon in Tanis and to Hori-Hor at Waset (Thebes), Egypt was not what it used to be. From this period we have been given *The Instructions of Amenemope*, which were important for Magon and me when we edited a section for *Proverbs*, but things have not been good in Egypt. Finally during David's reign here, Siamon came to power in Egypt, and he just may have helped David to control the Philistines. In fact, he captured and destroyed Gezer. That is the background for what I must tell you. Now there is a second Psusennes who rules in Egypt. Solomon and Psusennes have been negotiating for just a short time concerning a political marriage, and I have been involved in these talks.

"Psusennes is now willing to give his daughter to be Solomon's wife, and he is willing to give Gezer as her dowry. I don't know the name of this woman. At first I thought it was Ma'ka-Re', but I was wrong. She has a young sister by that name. But Solomon will soon bring his new wife here, and she will be housed in David's palace until Solomon can build a new palace. I don't know why Solomon needs another palace, but that is the plan.

"Magon I wanted you to hear this, because when we worked with *The Instructions of Amenemope,* we called it *A Handbook for Diplomats.* I have found out in these negotiations that it contains wise teachings. One passage was especially helpful. I will give our version of it:

> When you sit down to dine with a ruler,
> Consider carefully who is before you,
> And you should put a knife to your throat,
> If you are one who possesses an appetite.
> Do not desire his tasty foods;
> He and [the] food are deceptive."
> (Proverbs 23:1–3)"

Magon said, "I remember that passage well, but I'll bet that you did not need to recall it. I think you are well trained in such things."

"Perhaps, but during the negotiations I found I had even forgotten some Egyptian. The words were sometimes as slow as sea snails. I could not retrieve some expressions that I wanted."

Well, we had a long evening. Everyone had lots of questions not only about Solomon's Egyptian bride but also about his plans for a new palace and a temple for Yahweh. Father was concerned that all of this building would cost too much. I do not know when the party broke up, but Sharmila and I left before it did.

19

ALONG WITH SOLOMON'S NEW bride from Egypt came a new wave of building. This was all interesting, and it would be expensive. We knew what this meant: new taxes and forced labor. In addition to these problems, it was becoming clear that Solomon was in the process of changing the monarchy. In David's second coronation in which he became King of Israel as well as Judah there was a covenant as proposed by the elders of Israel and composed by Sheva according to our traditions. As father mentioned in his discussion of David's *Last Words*, this covenant was always conditional: David promised to keep the covenant and his sons in turn must do the same in order for the Davidic line to continue. But In David's *Last Words*, he does not speak of a conditional covenant but rather an *eternal covenant*. This represents a big change, and Solomon seems to be pushing ahead with the idea that the covenant is eternal and unconditional—he and his sons can do as they please because the House of David is eternal. As father put it last evening, "I think we must be watchful with Solomon as our king." I remember these words, because as it turned out they were prophetic.

A few days later, father came by to see me in my office. Acting in his capacity as head of the academy, he was passing out some work assignments. Father said, "Naam, I have an interesting project for you. As you know I have been working on David's chronicles, and at the same time I must see to it that Solomon's chronicles are kept up to date. We do not have much on Solomon as yet, but already we have a little notation that makes some suggestions as to the extent of his wisdom or at least what should be credited to him as our king. Father left the note with me, and asked me to look at it and find some material to expand it if possible. Here is the text:

> Elohim gave Solomon wisdom. Solomon spoke concerning the trees, from the cedar that is in Lebanon to the hyssop that comes out from the wall. He spoke about the domesticated animals, about the birds, about the reptiles, and about the fish. (1 Kings 5:9a and 13 [English 4:29a and 33])

This short list of some areas of Solomon's expertise is interesting but not helpful. But perhaps I am wrong. This is a rather familiar "Table of Contents" for a *Royal Farmer's Almanac*, which is an essential item in the collections of documents in any royal center or a scribal school library. Such things are important for training those who care for horses and for others who produce food and wine for all of us, and the king or ruler always gets the credit for knowing how to deal with all of these subjects. Magon has talked about such manuals among his people at Tyre, which they inherited from Ugarit. Also, a farmer's calendar was usually included in such works. I recall that in our oldest traditions we even looked at our ancestors as great farmers. In our *Royal Epic* we do not hear much about Isaac, but the story about his sojourn in Gerar contains a note about his knowledge of farming:

> Isaac sowed in that land.
> He reaped in the same year a hundred [measures] of barley.
> Yahweh blessed him.
> The man became great; he continued growing until he was very great.
> He had a flock of sheep, a herd of cows, and a large labor force.
> The Philistines hated him.
> And all the wells that the servants of his father had dug
> (in the days of Abraham, his father),
> the Philistines ruined them; they filled them with dirt.
> (Genesis 26:12–15)

I really do not know as yet how to expand on this. I will just have to set it aside, and perhaps I can expand it later.

20

MY FATHER'S WORRIES INCREASED at a rapid pace. As head of the academy he had too much contact with Solomon's administration in the form of interference with his work on the chronicles. About five years after the death of David, father's health was on the decline; he was sixty-five. His workdays became shorter and as he put it, "It is hard to describe one's mood when we face old age as options fade. No use to be mad, but it is easy to be sad."

My father did enjoy my sisters, Ruth and Elissa; they were now eighteen and twenty-one, and they helped in the academy school for faculty children. My mother also worked there at times. Elissa was in love with Joel. They met five years ago at our wedding. Joel is a fine fellow and a good scribe. Ruth corresponds with Jacob, who was one of the scribes working for Abdianati in Beth-shan. Joseph, the other scribe, who was in Beth-shan, married Sharmila's sister, Huraya, about a year ago. By this time Sharmila and I had two children, and mother and father loved them dearly. Our girl we named Deborah, and our boy we named Noah. They are great kids. I should also mention that Khety and Tamar also had two children by this time.

I do not know how much time I have to finish my story, and I am getting nervous; there is a long road ahead, and I can see that I will have to summarize the main events of Solomon's reign and some of the major events in my family's story. I want everyone to know about what my family and our friends accomplished, but some of the events are sad; they are too painful to dredge up in great detail. My main concern is to show how our work at The Jerusalem Academy enabled us and our students to experience the beauty and the richness of our world. We lived in a small state, but we were able to see beyond our borders and appreciate the view. At the same time, we were concerned about Solomon. He seemed to be interested in building a great state with its great city, namely Jerusalem, but he has also shown that he can be ruthless.

As I have mentioned before, Solomon's building program called for heavy taxes and forced labor. But as I heard today Solomon cannot pay his bills. Samuel stopped by my office. I welcomed him and asked about Rachel. He said that she was fine as were the children, but he was eager to fill me in on some news. He had recently visited his parents in Shechem. He said, "There are many people in the north or the House of Joseph who are having problems with Solomon's taxes, and they are extremely angry about Solomon's forced labor; they are bearing the main burden of this policy. One of my old friends, Jeroboam ben Nebat, came to see me during my visit, and he told me all about this situation. In addition, he said that Solomon has put him in charge of the forced labor from the House of Joseph. Jeroboam is a capable person. He can do his job, but he is already wondering if he should be working for Solomon. He is forced to put people he has known to work on Solomon's projects—this is difficult for him—but on the other hand, he thinks that perhaps he can make things better for them. He is a bit confused."

"He has a difficult task," I said, "and I hope that he can help his friends without getting into serious trouble with Solomon."

"Jeroboam and other friends told me that Solomon's building program is so huge that Solomon is the one who is in trouble. When you build a temple for Yahweh, a palace for yourself and another for your Egyptian wife, and new city walls, it takes lots of wealth and labor. Also Solomon has added to this program by initiating the rebuilding and fortifying Hazor, Megiddo, and Gezer. In addition, he is fortifying outposts, supply depots, and bases for chariots and horses. He has recently purchased hundreds of chariots and horses. He gets most of the horses from Kue in the far north, even north of ancient Ugarit. They are good horses, and he has even employed people from Kue and some from Tyre to help train and care for these horses. At Tyre they keep some manuals on the care of horses that they inherited from the veterinarians of ancient Ugarit. I relate these details to make my point that Solomon is spending, spending, and spending again. It seems that King Hiram of Tyre is also angry with Solomon. Years ago Solomon and Hiram cut a deal, but now Solomon is not keeping his part of it. Hiram agreed to supply Solomon with timber for his building projects, both cedar and cypress; he also supplied him with gold. Solomon also used Hiram's stonemasons to help shape quarried blocks of stone. For this Solomon was to make an annual payment of food, both wheat and olive oil. It now seems that Solomon could not make these payments, and so he gave Hiram twenty cities in the western region of Galilee. But after seeing the cities, Hiram was not pleased with them."

I said, "I have also heard about these cities Solomon gave to Hiram. This 'gift' is in fact a strip of land whose southern border runs from Acco in the west to Kabul in the east, and at that width it goes north to Tyre. Hiram may not have been pleased with the cities, but I imagine he is pleased with such a buffer strip to protect his coastal ports. Solomon is able to pay his debt in this manner, and while complaining, Hiram gets what he wants."

"You may be correct, because somehow it appears that Hiram and Solomon have settled some of their problems. Now they are going into the shipping business. Jeroboam thinks Hiram, who controls most of the shipping on *hayyam haggadol*, "the great sea," wants to expand his business to the south and the east—to Ophir and beyond. In order to do this he would need overland access to Solomon's port, Ezion-geber, and the Reed Sea.

"But I have strayed from my main point. I want to stress that Solomon's taxes and forced labor may just be our downfall. I do not know what we can do, but somehow we need to help Jeroboam if he gets into trouble."

"I will discuss some of this with my father," I said, "but it will not be easy for us to help."

"But somehow we must. If our country is torn apart, those of us from the north, who are in this academy, would have to return to Shechem. I would hate to see such a thing."

"So would I. Thanks for sharing these things, and I will do anything that will help."

After Samuel left I went to father's office, and I talked at length about all of this. Father said, "I have seen this coming for some time. Solomon thinks he can do anything he wants, because he says that he has an unconditional blessing from Yahweh. Nathan is also claiming this for Solomon. This is no surprise, because he claimed the same for David, and his oracle inspired David to believe that his House is eternal. In Nathan's oracle he tells David that after David's death, Yahweh will establish the kingship of his son. If that son does wrong, he will be punished just as other humans, but Yahweh will not remove his favor from the son. Yahweh concludes:

> Your house and your kingdom shall remain secure forever before me,
> and your throne shall be established unto eternity. (1 Samuel 7:16)

Recently Nathan has been telling me to remove all references to Yahweh's conditional covenant with David and Solomon in their chronicles. He does not want people to know that according to the covenant, David and Solomon must keep the laws and commandments if they want Yahweh's blessings. Well, I will not delete such references. Nathan supports the king regardless of what the king does. This change will tear us apart."

"I take it you mean both our state and our academy."

"Yes, and I suggest that you stay close to Samuel and keep up to date on what is happening with Jeroboam."

"I will do just that."

21

THE NEXT FIVE YEARS brought more difficulties. Most of the problems increased and surrounded us on every side. Only a few were solved. Nathan, first as David's royal prophet and later as Solomon's prophet, kept a great deal of pressure on father to re-write the chronicles with many deletions, and father resisted him daily. Father maintained that we have several chronicles, and each has a different point of view. The many voices are all important—even the voice of Nathan. Also, Solomon kept up his building program. Jeroboam was still in charge of the forced labor, but things were getting much more difficult. Solomon kept demanding more work and allowing less food and rest. He also wanted more workers, and this meant that the old and the young were no longer exempt. I heard every few days from Samuel who was always in touch with Jeroboam and his problems. One evening after dinner Sharmila and I talked about these problems. In fact Sharmila told me that she and Rachel had also been discussing most of these matters, and that Rachel thinks Jeroboam will not last much longer working for Solomon. If he is forced out, Samuel and Rachel will probably leave. They will go back to Samuel's home in Shechem. "Do you think this will happen?" she asked.

"It could," I answered, "because Solomon is determined to get what he wants. If Jeroboam cannot line up the workers, he will be in trouble, and Solomon could also go after Jeroboam's friends. In fact, he could also make things difficult for us."

"What do you mean?"

I took Sharmila in my arms and said, "I do not know what I mean. It all depends on what Jeroboam does. If he just quits his job, he will become an outcast, but if he attempts to enlist the support of others in the north, or old Israel, this would be taken as an act of rebellion. In this case, any friend of Jeroboam, like Samuel, would have to seek safety, and also I have been involved. I have not approved of the way Solomon has disrupted people's lives and caused hardship. I am convinced that Solomon does not understand or care about Jeroboam or the problems of those who have to leave their families and homes to work on his projects. Recently, Jeroboam allowed a young man to leave his place on a forced labor gang; he needed to help his widowed mother provide for her other children. She needed her son as she was in dire straits. But Solomon, upon hearing about this situation, reversed Jeroboam's decision. There are many stories like this."

"But your position in the academy is important. Would Solomon risk a move against you?" Sharmila asked.

"I think he would. After all he only cares about himself."

"If we had to leave, we could always go to my folks' place in Beth-shan."

"Yes, but also we might have to go to Tyre in order to continue our work in progress. Magon's sister is there and the academy at Tyre is an interesting place as your father knows so well."

During these hard times, we had other bad news. Sheva died. This was a real shock to many of us in the academy. Sheva had been important for all of us throughout David's reign, and Sarah helped bring me into this world. This meant that Sarah would come back to Jerusalem and live with her daughter. Naomi and Magon would welcome her, but what will Solomon do with Sheva and Sarah's land grant? I hope it stays with Naomi and Magon. We all attended Sheva's funeral, which was held in Jerusalem.

In the midst of all this difficulty my father had horrible chest pains and died two days later. What a blow to our family, our friends, and the academy. He was the greatest of fathers, and my mother and my father were an extraordinary couple and a team beyond compare. They gave direction to our personal existence, and this in turn, had an impact on friends and the academy. What would mother do? Obviously, she will take care of her girls, Elissa and Ruth, plus she will remain concerned about our family and friends. I suspect she will continue to write and remain interested in the academy and the future role of Solomon. Solomon, with the help of Nathan, might be able to shape many of our documents according to his views.

All of us were wondering who would head the academy with Sheva and father gone. We would have to wait and see. At the moment it was more important to take care of mother and my sisters, and we had to arrange father's funeral at his tomb in Bethlehem. His friends and the men of his Beth Marzeah, or house of mourning, would help us as they did when we buried my grandfather and the scroll of *The Rebel Job*. In fact, Elhanan, one of father's closest friends, offered to help us as soon as he heard the news. I have already mentioned that Elhanan was the one who actually killed Goliath, though he never objected to the story that credited David with the feat.

I arranged for a donkey and cart to transport father's body to Bethlehem, and the rest of us gathered at our house just as the sun was rising for a good breakfast before we set out on foot for Bethlehem. Elissa and Ruth helped Sharmila and me with our children, Deborah and Noah. Mother, Sharmila and I were busy serving our breakfast guests. Magon and Naomi, along with Sarah, Khety and Tamar, Elishama and Deborah, and Rachel and Samuel, also helped us with the breakfast. These couples, our closest friends, had brought with them everything that we would need for lunch. We were all planning to eat dinner and stay the night at the Beth Marzeah. We would have the burial for father early the next morning, and then after breakfast we would begin our return trip. The trip was difficult for Sarah, because she had just buried Sheva, and I think she was about seventy-five at the time. That would be right, because she was five years older than father. Mother was sixty-three and in good health, but for her, this trip was too sudden; it was unbelievable; her soul mate was gone.

We had a good lunch and there was plenty of time to rest, remember, and shed a few tears. As we were eating, mother said through her tears, "I remember stopping here for lunch when we were going to Bethlehem to bury the scroll of *The Rebel Job*. Jonathan told the group that in this area Jacob had set up a pillar at the grave of Rachel. She had died giving birth to Benjamin. He noted that the pillar is gone but not so the memory of the mother of Joseph and Benjamin. Jonathan loved to remember such events and to place them for us where we stood. I understand that better as I remember him standing by this large flat rock where we have spread our lunch."

Magon said, "The place of a significant event can send a chill down my spine, but your words, as a participant in the event, make my experience even better and beyond description. Keziah, I thank you for recreating a great moment."

22

WE HAD A WONDERFUL dinner at the Beth Marzeah. Jonathan's friends under the direction of Elhanan fixed this for us, and after dinner they brought in some musicians. We listened and we sang. The children liked this time of singing together. We were all tired, and so we soon spread out our blankets and went to sleep.

We were up with the sun and were soon gathered at Jonathan's tomb. Mother had asked me to lead our small group in the funeral ritual. Sharmila and I stood before the tomb, and I began with the summoning of our ancestors.

"We call forth the names of our ancestors that they may give us their blessings: Abraham and Sarah, Isaac and Rebekah, Jacob, Leah, and Rachel, and Judah and Tamar, who gave us Perez, Hezron, Ram, Amminadab, Nahshon, Salmon, and Boaz. Next, we call forth the names of Boaz and Ruth, who gave us Obed, who was the father of Jonathan, our loving father. In addition, in this setting it is time to call forth both Jonathan and mother's parents, Gad and Jael."

Mother, Elissa, and Ruth stepped forward and in unison called forth their names: "We call forth your names Gad, Jael, and Jonathan, and we seek your blessings."

Now it was time to remember my father, Jonathan. I asked our friends to speak first, and after them, the family members.

Magon got up first and said: "This is a time to remember. I remember our times together at the funeral of Ahban, of Gad, and of the rebel Job. On these occasions Jonathan's remarks were always important for me. I cannot be as eloquent as Jonathan, but I hope to be truthful and passionate about Jonathan's enduring value to his friends, his family, and to the academy. Jonathan's vision was important in the early years of our academy. He invested a great amount of energy in making the academy a cosmopolitan center of learning. Hear us Jonathan; we thank you.

"Jonathan, along with Elishama and Elimelech, performed an almost impossible job of putting together *The Royal Epic of Israel*. Other countries have some great stories, but they have not brought them together in this form. Hear us Jonathan; we thank you.

"Next, I speak of his greatest work, *The Rebel Job*. This wonderful poem addresses the problems of human existence in a new way. Others have attempted to deal with such problems without success. The rebel argues against the orthodox doctrine of retribution: the just are rewarded and the evil ones suffer and perish. The rebel maintains that this doctrine is false, and there is no justice. Elhanan has engraved some words of the rebel on this stone beside me: 'Seek not justice but help the poor.' Jonathan's poem becomes the rule by which all orthodox positions and traditions should be judged. Jonathan has helped all of us. Hear us Jonathan; we thank you.

"Jonathan's work is priceless, but I remember him most for his constant openness to his friends. In this he followed Gad, whose table was always a place of good food, laughter, entertainment, and helpful words of wisdom. There is no doubt that Jonathan was also a loving husband and father. Jonathan and Keziah and their understanding of what it means to be one has been indispensable for Naomi and me. Hear us Jonathan; we thank you."

Elishama was next, and he said, "At Gad's funeral, I remember saying that whenever Gad attended our work sessions on *The Royal Epic of Israel* he made an important contribution. Therefore, it was clear to me why Jonathan looked to Gad, his father-in-law, as his teacher. Jonathan's openness to others made him an insightful teacher, and he was my teacher. As we worked together he did not coerce. He gathered material to support his point of view, and he persuaded Elimelech and me to follow. But if we came up with materials that suggested an alternative view, he was quick to make a change in his thinking. Jonathan was a special human being. He cannot be replaced; he can be remembered with thanks."

Khety said, "I certainly agree with all that has been said here today. In addition, I would like to emphasize that Jonathan's *Rebel Job* will put his name on the lips of many, from Egypt in the south to the land of the Hittites in the north. In most of the countries that surround us, many have tried to deal with the difficulties that surround humans and other creatures; they have all failed. We live in a beautiful setting, but it can expose us to hardships. Plus, we are mortals. Jonathan did not make the mistake of others by blaming the gods for hardships and disasters. He did not put the blame on the sins of nations or of individuals. He did not resort to the idea of retribution. Rather than any of these old and worn out approaches and knowing that looking for justice is a hopeless task, Jonathan taught us that it is essential to love and help the powerless. Helping others to cope with tragedy makes appreciation of the beauty of our earth a real possibility. Jonathan was creative; he came up with something new. He has helped us, and he will help many others in years to come."

Sarah raised her hand, and I said, "Sarah come on up here."

But Sarah said, "I'll stay right here, but I must say that Jonathan helped to reunite my family. Sheva was always so grateful for all that Jonathan did for the academy and for us personally. He was always helpful."

Naomi stood up and said, "I must add to mother's thanks. Jonathan was there for us, but he would be the first to say that Keziah also helped to mend the breach between my father and me. Jonathan and Keziah knew how to work as one."

"Thank you Sarah and Naomi," I said, "and I will always be thankful for Sarah's help. She helped bring me into this world."

At that point mother stepped forward and said, "Naam, I can remember what you said at your grandfather's funeral. You closed your comments with these words, 'I could say much more about grandfather, but I cannot say it now. My tears are washing away my words.' I feel the same way when I try to talk about Jonathan. But I can say one thing. We were bound together, and yet we were at the same time free. I thank all of you for your support."

Finally it was my turn, and I said, "I thank all of you for your participation in this moment of farewell. I have talked with all of you, and I know we are all aware of a great personal loss with the passing of my father. That is foremost on my mind. I also know that father would want us to think in terms of the future, but we can talk about that later. I am going to miss our table talk. We shared our day's work, problems, and discoveries. This was not just a conversation between my father and me; it involved every member of our family. Father helped us work out our problems, but his help came in the form of a suggestion. We knew what he preferred in most situations, but there is one most important thing about father: he trusted us. He often made suggestions, but he would step back and allow us the freedom to act. Indeed, he trusted us.

"We will be able to recall many other things as we return to Jerusalem, so I will end with our traditional blessing:

Shalom!
Shalom to Jonathan!

Shalom to Keziah, Ruth, Elissa, and Naam!
Shalom to the grandchildren!
Shalom to the academy!
Shalom to her teachers and their families!
Shalom!

23

WE RETURNED TO THE Beth Marzeah where Elhanan informed me that the members of the Marzeah had packed some lunch for us. Elhanan had put it on a donkey. He would go with us until we reached a good place for lunch, and after lunch, he would return to Bethlehem with the donkey. As we started on our walk, I made a point of walking with Elhanan. I thanked him for all that he had done over the years for us. He said, "Your father was not only my closest friend, but he was also my best and truest friend. He never asked for the impossible, only asking for my help in order to help others. I will miss him."

"I appreciate your kind words," I said, "and I hope that I will be able to help you some day. We are all worried about what Solomon is going to do now that father is gone. He would like to change some of our chronicles, and cover up anything that detracts from David's reputation or his. Also his treatment of the forced labor gangs might lead us into troubled times."

Elhanan responded, "I have heard many complaints about the forced labor. But I have other concerns. Solomon has threatened me concerning the death of Goliath. Jonathan told me that you knew that I was the one who actually killed Goliath. Well, Solomon wants me to issue a statement that I killed the brother of Goliath. This is another one of his cover-ups. I see no need to do this, because I have never talked about killing Goliath. David can have the glory."

"But you must be careful. Solomon can be cruel. I will let you know if I hear anything about his intentions concerning you."

We had a great lunch, and everyone thanked Elhanan for his kindness. As he left to return to Bethlehem, we all wished him well. We rested for a while longer and noticing mother was caring for our children, I walked over to her and asked how she was holding up. She said, "I'm fine, and it does help to be in such good company."

"Well let me know when you want relief from the burden of the children."

"Everything is fine."

So I went over to where Sharmila was visiting with Rachel and Samuel. I wanted to rest just a little and to talk with Samuel, and so I joined them. I said to all three, "I think I have neglected you folks today."

Rachel said, "You have, but we sort of understood that you were busy."

Sharmila said, "Come and sit down. This is a nice place beside me."

I bent over and gave Sharmila a kiss, and said, "I'll just take that place, and yes, I have been busy, and perhaps it is a good thing. Father would probably tell me to stay busy and look ahead."

"He would also approve of what you are doing right now," Sharmila added. "You enjoy spending time with your friends."

We had a good visit, and finally I asked Samuel, "Have you heard any more from Jeroboam?"

"I hear from him at least once a week, and things are getting worse, week by week."

"How so?"

"Solomon's people are issuing false statements. They maintain that only foreigners are made into slaves, and that no one from Israel is made to be a slave. But believe me, if you are a member of a forced labor gang, you are a slave. You may be sent to Lebanon to move cedar logs or to the quarries to bring out huge blocks of stone. You work hard, and even if you are needed at home, you will not receive an exemption. It is difficult for Jeroboam to be a part of this and have to listen to lies. After all, he is a *gibbor hayil*, 'a mighty man of valor.' He is a landed property owner, and as such owes military service and taxes to the king, but he is being asked to bring suffering upon his people. He was chosen by Solomon to oversee the forced labor of the House of Joseph, because he was a somebody, not a nobody. He thought he might be able to help his people, but this has become impossible."

"So what will he do?"

"He does not know as yet. He has a difficult problem. Some workers have escaped from their work places and returned home, and they are in hiding. Others disappear before they are called up. Most of the people like Jeroboam, and they are urging him to resist Solomon's orders to provide more workers. If he stands with his people, Solomon will seek to kill him, and if he obeys Solomon the people will not only suffer more hardship, but they will turn away from Jeroboam."

"Solomon will seek to kill him if he has a following. This will be understood as rebellion."

Rachel and Sharmila were listening to this conversation, and they both looked worried. Rachel said, "Every time I hear about this, I feel our situation is becoming very dangerous."

I said, "This situation may indeed cause all of us and the academy a lot of trouble, but we will help in every possible way. We should make some plans for any emergency in the future. In the near future you folks should come over to our house, and we will do some planning. Right now I think we need to get on our way. I note that others are packing up."

With that Sharmila and I went over to help mother with the children. We all had an enjoyable walk back to Jerusalem.

24

WHEN WE GOT HOME, we were tired. We spent part of the next day putting things back in order, but Sharmila and I spent most of the day with mother. It was not going to be easy for any of us to get used to life without father. On our second day at home, I went to my office, but I spent most of the time talking to Magon about Jeroboam. We also talked about who should become the new head of the academy. We thought Elishama would be a great leader, but he might want to return to Shechem if the Jeroboam situation gets worse. But Magon said that we should try to convince him to stay here. After all, he is not a close friend of Jeroboam; Samuel's situation is different. We need Elishama, and he is almost finished with Part Two of *The Royal Epic.* Magon added, "Elishama is certainly my choice. We cannot allow Jonathan's detractors or Solomon's 'faithful servants' to take over. Elishama would also keep northern traditions alive regardless of what happens in the future. Also, he has always been interested in the unity of Judah and Israel. His work on Part One of *The Royal Epic* helped to bring about this greater Israel, and he is essential to the academy now and in the future."

We decided to have a talk with Elishama, and if he agreed to take the leadership position, we would take the necessary steps to make it happen. This would not be difficult. Everyone likes Elishama.

After about two weeks Elishama agreed to become the head of the academy, and in another two weeks we had convinced the faculty that Elishama would be a great leader. He knew all the materials we had used in our *Royal Epic*, and he had always been fair in his treatment of northern and southern traditions. He was able to relate to the other teachers even when he disagreed with them. I was fearful that Solomon or Nathan would object to our selection, but the administration went along. I think Solomon believed that since Elishama was from the north it might help the situation in the north to promote one of their own. The northern people were rightly complaining: they were being mistreated, they had to pay excessive taxes, and they had to send more of their sons to the forced labor gangs. Perhaps this promotion of Elishama would win some friends in the north. For whatever reason Solomon went along. This made us all feel a bit better, and we were able to return to our work and teaching with some hope for the future.

Soon after, Elishama came to see me in my office. He reported that Nathan had already been pushing him to eliminate some of the chronicles. I said, "This is what he was always doing to father, but father told him that we need all of these chronicles. I think you can try your best to ignore Nathan. He has not been quite so bad since we accused him of stealing Gad's work on David from father's office. I think we told you that my mother has copies of Gad's work, so we still have them whenever you need one. When I was working on *The Journey of Wen-Amon*, I was pleased to note that Zakar-Baal, Prince of Byblos, also found that the old Byblos chronicles were very important and useful. At one point Wen-Amon says, 'Then he ordered his ancestors' *Scrolls of the Days*, and he had them read in my presence. They found entered one thousand *deben* of silver (and) all sorts of things in his scrolls.' Zakar-Baal used these chronicles to prove his point in his negotiations with Wen-Amon. Our neighbors have kept their chronicles and used them to their advantage. We must do the same. Solomon and Nathan just do not understand. Our many chronicles will help us in the future. These two can write their propaganda pieces if they so desire, but that does not mean that they can destroy our chronicles. Obviously, they want to promote their point of view and destroy the evidence for other views and assessments. So we will have to keep our chronicles in a safe place."

"Are you suggesting that we should hide them," Elishama asked with hesitation in his voice.

"I am, and as you know this is not difficult to do. Our main difficulty in this academy is to find things that we have put somewhere for safe keeping."

"As you speak, I can hear your father. If Jonathan were here, he would make the same point that you have expressed. Also, I know a lot about trying to find things. Jonathan kept us busy finding stories for our *Epic*. I think I can handle this. Thanks. I also want to thank you for discussing some of Samuel and Rachel's problems with them. I am hoping that they can stay here, but I understand that Samuel is too close to Jeroboam to avoid trouble if Solomon finds it necessary to punish Jeroboam. Rachel and Samuel are getting ready to leave if they are forced into exile."

"That would be a sad day for all of us. I hope Solomon does not continue on his present course. He is not helping himself, the kingdom, or anyone."

After Elishama left, I thought to myself, "Elishama is going to be good for this academy."

I started on some preparations for my classes, but it was not easy to put Elishama's visit out of my mind. Also, I was beginning a translation of a great Egyptian story, *The Eloquent Peasant*, and I was having some problems, and so I decided to go see Khety, who is always is willing to help. Entering his office, I was happy to see that he was there. He welcomed me with his gracious smile, but still it seemed to me that he was troubled. He soon told me all about what was worrying him. Khety said, "I just got back from the palace. Solomon keeps asking me to help with his correspondence with Egypt. While I was there I overheard Solomon dictating a document to a palace scribe. Now that Sheva has died he is taking back the royal land grant to Sheva and Sarah and giving it to Benaiah. Tamar and I thought that Solomon would grant Sheva's land to someone else, but we never expect him to give it to Benaiah, the head of the army. This will certainly remove that sense of freedom we have always felt when we were at Tamar's land grant. Tamar is not going to like this."

"I am sorry to hear this. This puts everything back as it was when Joab had that grant, and he was not a good neighbor."

"Right, and Banaiah will present us with some of the same problems. He will be the eyes and ears of Solomon!"

"This is not good. I should tell you that there are other problems that are beginning to surface. Jeroboam is a close boyhood friend of Samuel, and he has been in charge of the forced labor gangs from the north. However, he is finding out that he is in no position to help his friends in the north. In fact, Solomon is asking him to hurt, rather than help, his friends. If Solomon turns against Jeroboam, Samuel and Rachel may have to leave us. I have been thinking, up to now, that if they need to escape, they could spend the first night at Sheva and Sarah's place. However, that is no longer a possibility."

"Your father told me about this shortly before he died. Is this problem getting worse?"

"I think it is."

"Then we should make a plan that will help Samuel and Rachel, and we should not involve Elishama in any way. We need him here."

"Khety, can you and Tamar come to our house tomorrow evening? If so I will ask Samuel and Rachel to come over as well, and we will plan."

"We will be there."

Needless to say, I did not even mention my problems with *The Eloquent Peasant*. Those problems would have to wait for another day.

25

THE NEXT DAY SHARMILA arranged with Tamar and Rachel for all of us to have dinner together before our planning session. Ruth was going to take care of the children at Tamar and Khety's house, and mother and Elissa would join us for dinner and planning. It would have been good to have Magon and Naomi in the group, but they were busy helping Sarah move her things out of the estate that now belonged to Benaiah. Since Sarah would be living with them, they were bringing some of her things to their house; They would store other things at Tamar's place for the time being.

I left my office early in order to help with the preparations. Mother was helping as well, and it was good to see her and to work with her. She asked me to prepare a leg of lamb using the outside fire pit. I said to her, "I can remember when you were cooking lamb, years ago, for our first dinner and meeting with Khety, and many lambs later we are doing it again."

Mother said, "I remember that day as well. You were telling the girls a story, and I could not get you to finish and come down from the roof. But when you and the girls smelled the drippings hitting the coals, you soon came down to help with the dinner and get closer to the delicious aroma."

"Ah yes, and that is why I am here now. Does your fire need attention?"

"I do not know. You had better check it."

When I went outside to check the fire, I noticed that Sharmila, Tamar, and Rachel were all outside working with the vegetables and fruit. They had already set out the cheese, bread, honey, and yogurt on the table. On the side table they had arranged the raisin cakes and wine. There was no doubt that everyone was having a good time. It is good to be together.

We had a great dinner, but I did miss father. He was always at his best with his friends and family around this table. After most of the food was put away, mother and Elissa served the raisin cakes and poured more wine. I asked Samuel to give us an update on Jeroboam's situation. Samuel said, "Jeroboam and I met early this morning, and I did receive the latest news. I usually meet him during an early morning walk, which we vary from week to week. Things are becoming more difficult, because the people in the north like him—after all he is a *gibbor hayil*, 'a mighty man of valor.' The fact that the people like him may just be his downfall. This may sound strange, but his loyal followers, who appreciate that he tries his best to help them, make Solomon anxious. Solomon is suspicious of anyone who has 'loyal followers,' and he equates this situation with rebellion. In fact, someone told Jeroboam that Solomon recently said, in the presence of several members of his administration, that Jeroboam has 'raised his hand' against me and my kingdom. Jeroboam is a rebel, but Benaiah knows what to do with rebels."

"So what is he planning to do?" asked Khety.

"He has already left for Edom. Friends are taking him to see Hadad, the Edomite prince who escaped to Egypt during David's reign. This happened during the time when Joab was killing the male children in Edom. Hadad was protected and raised by Pharaoh, and Pharaoh gave him land and his sister-in-law for his wife. After David's death, Hadad returned to rule in Edom. Jeroboam is quite certain that Hadad will help him get to Egypt and introduce him to Pharaoh."

"This is a surprise. I did not think this would happen so fast," Mother said.

Khety said, "It is my understanding that Pharaoh did not want Hadad to return to Edom and that Hadad's son remained in the Pharaoh's palace among his sons. Of course, things are different now with Shishak as Pharaoh. In Egypt he is called Sheshonq. But he will probably receive Jeroboam and care for him. But what does this mean for you, Samuel?"

"It means that we should leave at once. I have been too close to this event. But it also means that the north, or the House of Joseph, will have to endure more suffering. And even as Hadad had to remain in Egypt until David died, so Jeroboam will have to stay in Egypt until Solomon is dead; the suffering in the north will be prolonged. So the question for us is: how will we get out of Jerusalem and arrive safely at my folks' home in Shechem?"

Mother said, "Shechem is too close. Solomon will send his men there to look for Jeroboam's close friends and followers. He will also knock on the door of your folks. Perhaps you can get to your folks as a first step on your journey, but I suggest that you go on to Beth-shan and work with Sharmila's father."

Sharmila spoke up, "I think Keziah is right, and my folks would welcome you. Naam and I have talked about leaving as well, because he has also been close to Samuel through all of this. We have talked of visiting my folks, but Naam would really like to go to Tyre. Isn't that right Naam?"

"Yes, that is correct, and since Samuel has previously studied in Tyre, I would suggest that Samuel and Rachel could eventually come to Tyre as well. It would not be a difficult journey from Beth-shan. For now, I think mother has the right plan. Head north now, because Benaiah and his men are probably following Jeroboam's southern route."

Mother said, "I am surprised Naam that you are also thinking about leaving. Is Solomon also after you?"

"Perhaps not now, but everyone in this room could be involved in aiding Samuel and Rachel escape—especially me. I have been involved, and I do not regret it. That is why I do not think Khety and Tamar should be seen as helping hands in any of this. Also I think it is good that Magon and Naomi are not here and are not involved."

"Well, this is developing into a difficult situation," said Khety, "but we must put first things first. Our first task is to work on Samuel and Rachel's problem. We must get busy tomorrow and gather the supplies they will need, and Naam, you should find them a donkey for their supplies and one for their children. Rachel, you could gather up a few personal items, but you should take the rest of your things to your mother. I'm sure that Deborah can keep them for you."

Samuel said, "Some of my friends from Shechem who were here helping Jeroboam will be returning to Shechem tomorrow evening We could go with them. They are not known as Jeroboam's friends, and I think such a plan would work."

At that moment there was a loud knock on the door. As I opened the door three soldiers pushed their way into the room. We were all shocked and fearful. I said, "What is the meaning of this intrusion?"

The one who seemed to be in charge said, "Benaiah is on an important mission and has sent a message to us. He has ordered us to arrest a scribe by the name of Samuel. We are checking all of your living quarters."

Samuel stood up. "I am Samuel," he said. "Why does Benaiah want me?"

The other two soldiers grabbed Samuel, and the one in charge said, "You were seen recently at the Gihon spring talking to Jeroboam."

With that, the three soldiers took Samuel outside where a few more soldiers surrounded him, and they took him away. Shutting the door, I cursed, and mother ran over to Rachel. She held Rachel, who was crying uncontrollably and saying, "No, no, no."

Sharmila and Tamar were kneeling and holding Rachel's hands. I said to Khety, "So much for our plans. Khety, I think you and Tamar should go home and check on Ruth and the children. I will go and get Deborah, Rachel's mother, and then come to your house to get the children."

Mother saw us talking; asking Sharmila take her place, she came over to us. I told her what we were going to do. She said, "Yes, you should get Deborah, but don't bring the children back just yet. Rachel will need a little more time, and Khety, please take Elissa with you. She can help Ruth with the children."

Khety, Tamar, and Elissa left at once, but mother decided to go with me to get Deborah. They were such old friends, and mother wanted to break the bad news. After we arrived at Deborah and Elishama's house, mother told both of them what had happened. Mother gave Deborah some time to absorb the initial shock, and then she said to her, "We should go now, and you can comfort Rachel."

I stayed for a while and talked with Elishama explaining to him that he should not get involved with these problems. "We need you at the head of this academy," I said.

26

WE NEVER SAW SAMUEL again. One of his first-year Babylonian students somehow got word that Benaiah had him put to death. Benaiah was angry, because he had gone on a wasted mission; he never found Jeroboam. He had to get someone, and that someone was Samuel. Rachel and her two children moved back with her parents, and she decided to help her father with his work as head of the academy. Solomon sent a message to Elishama expressing his regrets, but Elishama did not reply. I did not know what to do. I wanted to send a letter of complaint to Solomon, but that would probably make things worse for everybody. About a week after Samuel's was taken from us, I had a talk with Magon.

Magon said, "If you plan to go to Tyre, you should do it soon. A large group of workmen from Tyre will be returning soon, and you could go with them."

"I might just do that, but it is difficult to decide what to do. I have to do what is best for my entire family and for the academy. If I wait too long, I might share the fate of Samuel, but I just do not know how I stand with Solomon."

Magon seemed to feel that I should not risk staying in Jerusalem, and Sharmila also thought that we should leave. If we were going, Mother and the girls wanted to go with us. As it turned out, our decision was not difficult. I received a message from Nathan in which he asked me to come to the palace to answer some questions concerning Samuel's connection with Jeroboam. Knowing that we could not trust Nathan in any situation, I did not answer him. Then Nathan sent a messenger to hand deliver his request. I told the messenger that I was not interested in answering Nathan's questions, and then I said, "Who does Nathan think he is? In this school we consider him a thief who stole my grandfather's scroll dealing with David. If he wants to ask me anything, he should come here in person."

The messenger said, "I should not be saying anything, but I knew your father, and your mother helped my mother. She gave my mother food when my brothers, sisters, and I were small and starving."

"Did you and your family go with us and eat lunch with us when we were on our way to Bethlehem a few years ago?"

"Yes we did, and I remember you from that day. You were all kind to us, and that is why I want to warn you that this could mean trouble. You should not confront Nathan on this. Nathan is helping Solomon round up many of Jeroboam and Samuel's friends. Others have declined to answer Nathan's questions, and they have disappeared. Their families have asked about them, but there is never an answer. You should not treat this lightly, and please forget me and my words."

"Thank you so much for this warning. I am writing on Nathan's message that I will come to the palace next week to see him. Please take this message back to Nathan, and again I thank you. Your secret is safe with me."

With that he left, and I went home to make plans with Sharmila and mother. When I got there mother was with Sharmila, and I told them at once that we would have to leave. Then I asked mother "Do you remembered the children, who were starving? You gave them food, and they also ate lunch with us on our way to Bethlehem."

She answered, "Of course I remember them. But why do you ask?"

"Because the messenger, who delivered a message to me from Nathan, was one of those you helped, and he, in return, helped me. He warned me that others who had responded to Nathan's questions were no longer around. I decided then and there: we must go. It helps to have friends."

"Yes, it does."

I told them that Magon had suggested that we leave along with some workmen, who were returning to Tyre. I said to Magon that I could check with the workmen to see when they were leaving, because I did not want to involve Magon in any of this. Mother said, "If we want to protect Magon, it might be better to just leave on our own."

Sharmila said, "I agree, and I would really like to go north to Bethshan and see my folks, before we go west to the sea and on up to Tyre."

I said, "This is just fine with me, and if anyone asks us about our trip we can say that it is a trip to see Sharmila's mother and father. I will go over to the school and see Amos. Every day he brings food from his garden to the academy. I can buy a couple of donkeys from him. But first, how long will it take us to get ready? We should leave as soon as possible."

"With the help of Ruth and Elissa, I could be ready by tomorrow evening," said Mother. "We will have to leave a lot of things here. Rachel will come over and get most of my scrolls and take them to the academy for safekeeping. Also I know that Elissa will want to see Joel before she leaves. I do not want to endanger him or us. So what do we do?"

"He should only come by here after dark as we prepare to leave. When I go to the academy, I will get a message to him. I will have Amos bring the donkeys tomorrow at noon. If I tie them behind the house they will not be seen. Sharmila, do you think we can be ready by tomorrow evening?"

"Yes I do, because I have been preparing for several days. I have been making extra bread, and we will need a lot of supplies. We will have seven to feed. When you see Amos, ask if we can get three donkeys and ask him to load one of them with some supplies from his garden."

Mother agreed with Sharmila, and I told them that I would try to get another donkey. Then I headed for the academy to speak with Elishama and to find Amos. As soon as I reached the academy, I went to Elishama's office, and I told him that we were preparing to leave. I said that things were just getting too dangerous here, and that we were planning to go to Bethshan to see Sharmila's parents and then on to Tyre. I promised that I would write to him from Tyre in a few months. I also said that Rachel would bring my mother's scrolls for him to keep. Then I told him that I was going to ask Amos for some donkeys and supplies. My final request was that he should compensate Amos from what the school owes me. He agreed to all of this and wished me well. Then he said, "If I need to send word to you for any reason, whom should I send with the message?"

"Send Joel, because Elissa will be in touch with him."

Then I went out to find Amos. He was behind the kitchen unloading some vegetables. He agreed to all my requests and said, "I will bring the donkeys in the late afternoon and help you load them. Then I will help you get started on a trail that will allow you to hit the main road to the north, just north of Gibeah. You will not be seen leaving Jerusalem. You will have some moonlight, and you should travel most of the night. The next morning you can rest off the road in the shade of a tree. I have followed this plan many times."

I thanked Amos, and I went by the library to find Joel. He was there, and after swearing him to secrecy, I told him our plan. Then I said, "Come to our house at dusk; Elissa wants to see you. We will be leaving as soon as it is dark."

Thanking him, I hurried home. When I got home I told everyone the plan and Elissa was overjoyed that Joel would come by at dusk. Then I said,

"This will be great, because we will avoid going by Benaiah's estate. Amos apparently goes this way to avoid being seen by those who might want to rob him of his goods. I started to tell Amos why we were leaving, but he stopped me. He did not want to know."

Sharmila said, "It all sounds good. Keziah and I came up with a plan. We will start early in the morning, and everyone has a list of things to do and things to pack. We even have a list for you, and the first thing on your list is 'office.' We mean you should get the things you need from your office, and we think you should do this now or at least pack your things, so that you can bring them to the house tonight or very early in the morning. We do not want to let anyone know what we are doing. We also shed a few tears over our plans; we want to be safe, but a journey into exile is not a happy trip."

"I am really sorry about this. Solomon has caused this tension and suffering throughout our country and especially in the north. But in spite of the tears, you have really been working, and I will go back now and pack up my office. If I finish before dark, I will come home and then return to get the things in the morning, but if it is dark when I finish, I will bring the bundles home."

When I got to my office, I saw Khety just going into his office. I walked over and knocked on his door and said to him, "We have to leave under cover of darkness tomorrow evening, so I would like to bring some manuscripts and texts to you for safekeeping. So I will be right back with them."

"When did you decide to leave?"

"We decided today. Nathan wanted me to come in for some questions, and I have learned that if I respond I might not be seen again. We must go."

"I am sorry to hear this. I will come to your office to get the manuscripts. This will save you some time."

We both went back to my office, and I loaded Khety up with about twenty scrolls. He said that he would come back for the rest. While he was gone I found some Egyptian texts that he had given to me. I wanted to keep *The Eloquent Peasant*, but the rest of them I would return to Khety. Also, I gave Khety the beginnings of my four-language dictionary. I did not take many scrolls for our trip. I did take my journals and some of my translations, but I would have to work in the library at Tyre for my future studies. When Khety came back, I said, "We will head north and go to see Sharmila's folks at Beth-shan. After that we intend to go to Tyre. I hope that you can visit us in Tyre, because I am quite certain that I will not be coming back to Jerusalem for a long time."

"I understand, and I want to visit Tyre."

"When you come, you should be prepared to stay for a few weeks, because I will have many questions for you. You have helped me so much in the past, and I will always be grateful."

With that Khety left, and since it was now dark, I picked up my bundles and headed for home.

27

THE NEXT MORNING WE started packing at daylight. It was a difficult task, because we could not take much with us. Always the question, "Is this essential?" was before us. Another question followed the first: "What to do with the things we were leaving?" Rachel was helping us, and she volunteered to take some of our better dishes to our close friends. Some lesser items she took for a few students in the academy, and she took most of mother's scrolls to Elishama's office. Mother kept her journals, *The Jerusalem Academy*, and *The Minority Report*. We would leave our houses empty for new teachers.

By the time Amos arrived with the donkeys, we were ready. We had carried all of mother's things over to our place, and it was easy to load the donkeys. Well, I should say that it was easy for Amos to load the donkeys. When we finished, the sun was just setting, and soon Joel arrived. Elissa ran into his arms, and the rest of us moved to the table. Mother and Sharmila served us our last meal in Jerusalem. Amos enjoyed the meal, but he did not let us linger long. We said our goodbyes.

We left our home at the academy compound, going down by the Gihon spring and proceeding north along a steep trail. It was not easy going, but we managed. Sharmila and I had packs, as did Ruth and Elissa. Our children, Deborah and Noah, who were now eight and ten, also had small packs. It was dark, but Amos knew the trail. He led with the donkeys, and I brought up the rear. We had to stop often to catch our breath. Amos told us that since the trail was steep the lazy robbers were not to be seen on it. In a few places the trail was narrow with a dangerous drop-off to our right. Now the moon was up, and it was easier now that we could see the trail. By the time the moon was overhead, we reached a level section of the trail. Amos stopped and said, "I think you can make it from here. The trail is much better; you have the moon; and you will hit the main road before moonset. If I were you, I would walk on until sunrise and then find a place to rest. I know that the children are tired, but just push on a bit more."

I thanked Amos and took his place at the head of our little caravan. We did hit the main road north of Gibeah, and by sunrise we were far to the north of Gibeah. When we thought it was safe, we went off of the road, where we found a group of three trees. We were all so tired that we went to sleep at once. But I did not sleep long; restless and alert I decided to rest and watch. By noon everyone was awake. After eating a quick lunch, we moved on. We needed to find water for the donkeys, and we knew we had to press on if we were to reach Beth-shan in four days.

Our trip was difficult in part, because we tried to be inconspicuous. When we approached a small village, mother and the girls would go first, and Sharmila, the children, and I would follow at some distance. Mother made things easier; she had a great talents, always finding a well or whatever we needed at the time. After we left the town, we would regroup. A couple of times while we were in our off-road rest, we saw soldiers on the road, and once in a village we turned down an alley to avoid them. I do not think that Benaiah pursued us. He may have gone to Bethlehem to find us. In any case our trip was difficult but uneventful. We did arrive in Beth-shan in four days.

Sharmila was happy to see her folks. Her father, Abdi-anati, was doing well, and her mother, Pidray was excited to see her. Sharmila congratulated her sister, Huraya. She said, "I understand that you are a married woman now. Will Joseph be here for dinner?"

Huraya said, "Yes, and he will bring Jacob along and that should make Ruth happy."

Ruth was obviously happy and nervous. I think Elissa felt a little left out with Joel still in Jerusalem.

Pidray said to mother, "Keziah, it is so good to see you. I am sorry that you had to leave your home, but we will help in any way we can. Sharmila wrote to us several months ago that they might have to leave, but I did not know that you would be with them."

"Well, I talked with the girls, and the three of us decided we did not want to stay in Jerusalem. We all thank you for receiving us and for your offer of help. We just hope that you do not get into any trouble for helping us."

Abdi-anati said, "I do not think we will get in any trouble. Solomon has not paid any attention to us. That is both bad and good. It is bad, because we need some help, but it is good that he does not vigorously collect taxes or seize our sons for his forced labor."

This sounded like we had come to the right place, and it was wonderful to rest in the shade, even though it was hot, and to eat regular meals.

We had a wonderful dinner, and in part, Sharmila and I relived the past. Yes, we did have melon, and Sharmila brought me a slice with a smile and a kiss.

After dinner, I said to Abdi-anati, "We have been busy preparing for our trip and then walking, but now that we can relax, I think it will soon be apparent to us that we were forced to leave our homes and what we loved. We are exiles. My father's poem concerning the rebel Job continues to live, or perhaps, has come alive once again. There *is* no justice. In the poem Job urges everyone to help the powerless. We have tried to do just that, but now we are the powerless. I know it will be difficult, but after we rest for a while, I want to go to Tyre and continue my writing. I believed it is important to sift our traditions, to improve our minds, and to extend our horizons."

Abdi-anati said, " Stay here and rest, and then I will help you get to Tyre. What you are doing is important for you, your family, and also for the academy. Solomon will not live forever. But now you and your family need to rest. We will see you in the morning."

As we were getting ready for bed, I said to Sharmila, "It is nice to be back here where we met. I remember the melon, but even more, I remember your beauty and how you made me feel. I want to make love tonight, something we could not do when we first met."

Sharmila smiled and said, "I thought about you most of that night twenty years ago, but tonight we can make love and go to sleep."

28

THE NEXT MORNING, I suggested that we take a look at the old city on top of the *tel*. I wanted to show my family the stela of the Egyptian Pharaoh Seti, which I had copied when father, Khety, and I came here on that first trip. Everyone agreed, and so we started climbing the *tel*, as it was still cool. On the way up, Elissa asked me, "How long ago was it when Seti ruled here?"

"About three hundred years ago, and after Seti, Rameses ruled. During their rule, the Egyptians hired mercenaries from the Sea Peoples, who came from the far west—that is, from Caphtor (Crete) and Alashiya (Cyprus). These people were related to the Philistines, and they stayed here for many years after the Egyptians left. The mercenaries left and probably joined with the Philistines shortly before David became our king. So Beth-shan was under Egyptian and foreign rule for a long time."

We had a good time looking at this very old city, and the children were excited to see it. They found small fragments of painted pottery left by the mercenaries from the west. After several hours of exploring it was getting too hot, so we went back to Abdi-anati's house. There we rested in the shade until lunch.

After about two weeks of hiking, resting, and great conversation, we started to make plans to move on to Tyre. In fact Sharmila, mother, Abdi-anati and I were sitting at a table in the yard discussing our plans when we had a troublesome surprise. Elissa approached us in tears, and Joseph and Jacob were helping Joel, who could barely walk. They sat Joel down just as Ruth arrived with some water. Mother poured some water and instructed Joel to drink slowly just a little bit at a time. We waited a while and finally, Joel was able to speak. He said haltingly, "Elishama ask me to bring you a message. I guess I ran too much, and I did not drink or sleep enough."

"Do you want to rest or do you feel well enough to give us the message?" Mother asked.

"I'm well enough. Elishama wanted all of you to know that Benaiah came looking for Naam at the academy. Elishama told Benaiah that he had not seen Naam for several days. Then Benaiah got angry, and he said that they had looked for Naam in Bethlehem without any luck. Then he asked Elishama, 'Do you suppose that he went to Beth-shan to visit his in-laws?' Elishama told Benaiah that he did not know. Benaiah left in an angry mood, saying that he would have to send some troops to Beth-shan to look for Naam. I did not see any of his troops on my journey, but I cannot be certain. Perhaps they are still on their way."

I said, "I thank you for your tremendous effort to bring us this message. I suggest that you get something to eat and get some rest. If we leave, you will need to go with us. It would be too dangerous for you to return to the academy."

Elissa and the others took Joel into the house, and they got him something to eat.

Abdi-anati said, "I cannot imagine that the troops are already here. Troops take their time, and we would have seen them if they were here. However, I think we should start getting you folks ready to leave. Joel will not be ready to leave tonight, but he should be ready by tomorrow night. If so, I will take you tomorrow night to a friend, who lives in Yeno'am, which is north of here at the southern end of Lake Chinnereth. You should go northwest from here to Kabul and then west to Acco. From Acco you can go north to Tyre. I am suggesting this route, because from Acco on up to Tyre you will be in land that belongs to Hiram, since Solomon gave the twenty cities to Hiram."

"That sounds like a good plan," I said, but we will have to see if Joel is strong enough."

Mother said, "We have several things to discuss. Ruth wants to stay here with Huraya, and yes, she also wants to be near Jacob. I have talked with Pidray about this, and we think it will be good for all concerned. So if we include Joel, we will have the same number on the trip to Tyre as on the trip here."

I said, "I do not see any problems with that plan as long as you are pleased with it."

Sharmila said, "I think it will be good for both of the girls."

Abdi-anati said, "I believe the plan will work, but we should be careful. Tonight Joseph, Jacob, and I will take turns as watchmen. We do not want to be surprised by any soldiers."

Everything was quiet during the night. In the morning Joel was much better, and we all helped to get ready. We were going to leave after dark. I noticed that mother was spending a lot of time with Ruth, and that was understandable. Ruth was her youngest and a wonderful daughter. I made sure that our donkeys were getting well fed and watered. They just might have to do without for a few days.

We left on schedule and arrived in Yeno'am in about seven hours. Abdi-anati's friend, Barak and his wife, Arsay, welcomed us. They had a nice home not far from the lake, and he was a fisherman. He was also friendly and helpful. He had a small pen for the donkeys, and a beautiful yard where we soon found places to spread our blankets. Sleep encompassed us, and our worries were put to rest.

We got up in the morning and were introduced to the beautiful view of the lake. Barak's home was actually a little north of Yeno'am and hence the wonderful view. We had a wonderful breakfast with good bread and cucumbers in yogurt. Barak and Arsay were so kind. After we ate, Abdi-anati said that he needed to get back to Beth-shan. We all said our good-byes, and he left. We started getting ready to leave. After about an hour later, we were once again surprised; Abdi-anati returned. He was breathless, and Pidray was with him. She was extremely tired, tearful, and her hair was burned.

I told Elissa to get some water. She went to the house, and I ran to help Abdi-anati with Pidray. We brought her to the shade, and Barak came running out with the water. Pidray was weeping, and mother offered her a drink. Abdi-anati said to me, "Pidray has witnessed a tragedy for us and for you."

29

ABDI-ANATI CONTINUED, "WHEN I met Pidray on the road, she was crying and saying over and over again, 'Joseph, our Huraya, Jacob, and Keziah's Ruth, they have been killed—burned alive.' She had been walking since long before dawn, and she said that Solomon's soldiers came in the middle of the night. Apparently Pidray was sleeping outside near the garden. When she woke up the house was on fire. She ran to the house, but the fire was too hot for her to do anything. She ran to the front of the house, and on the ground she found Joseph. Still alive, he told her that the soldiers came to the house and called out 'Abdi-anati.' They called, 'Come out, and bring Naam, the rebel scribe, with you.' Then Joseph said that he came out, and immediately they shot him—an arrow to his chest. Then Joseph saw the soldiers setting the house on fire. It went up in flames, and the others could not escape. He heard the soldiers say, 'The rebel is surely dead. We can return to Jerusalem and get out of this heat.' Then Joseph said to Pidray, 'I have escaped, only I alone, to tell you.' But he did not escape; he soon died. That is about all I know, and I have not asked Pidray for any more information."

Sharmila was holding her mother in her arms; both were weeping. Elissa and mother were also weeping, and I was trying my best to comfort them. But I was really no help; I was awash in my own tears. Our children did not really understand what was going on. Barak, Arsay, and Joel were the helpful ones. They managed to get us all to the house. Then Arsay managed to get Pidray to eat some cucumbers and yogurt, and she told Sharmila, "Your mother must lie down and get some rest."

Arsay and Sharmila helped Pidray to get cleaned up and then put her in a bed. Then mother said to Elissa and to me, "We must allow our hearts to weep, but we need to talk about out situation. What will we do now?"

I said, "I am not sure that we have a choice. We must go on to Tyre. We cannot go back to Jerusalem, and we should not go back to Beth-shan. If everyone there thinks we are dead, so much the better. I know that I would like to go back to Beth-shan and hold funeral services there, but that is just not possible. We should have some kind of remembrance for Ruth and the others here and then move northwest to Kabul. I will speak to Abdi-anati, but I think that he and Pidray should come with us. In addition, I am worried about what our presence here with Barak and Arsay will do. I do not want to endanger them."

When I spoke to Abdi-anati about these matters, he thought we should move north, not staying any longer with Barak and Arsay. He agreed that he and Pidray should go with us, but he was not certain that they should go all the way to Tyre. He thought they might see if they could find a place to live in Kabul or perhaps in Acco where there was always a need for scribes. So we spoke to Barak about all of this. Barak was really not afraid. Arsay agreed with her husband, but she said that if we moved on north, we should leave Pidray for a few days of rest. Barak said, "I can take you north just a short distance to where my brother, Gideon, lives in Beth-yerah. You can stay there, and we will bring Pidray to join you in a couple of days."

I told mother and Sharmila of our new plans, and they agreed that it would be good to go to Beth-yerah, rest a bit, and hold a funeral service for Ruth and the others. Sharmila was thrilled with the idea that her folks would be going with us. It seemed to help our grief to be making plans, but nothing really helps for long. Solomon and Benaiah punished us through the actions of their soldiers and for what? They killed four innocent people, but then as the rebel Job taught us: there is no justice.

I could see that mother was hurting; Ruth was her youngest, and she loved her so much. Nevertheless, it was mother who pushed us to finish packing and to get started to Beth-yeah. Barak was ready to take us, and so we said good-bye to Arsay and Pidray. As we left, mother said, "This is such a beautiful setting. We received the horrible news of our tragedy here, but the beauty remains. We must help each other in the midst of tragedy to enjoy the beauty of our world even when we are surrounded with the suffering of the innocent. I really believe this even though the pain remains."

We soon arrived at Beth-yerah. It was close to the lake, and in some ways reminded us of Beth-shan. Years ago it had been a great and important city, but now there was only a small village. It was situated where the lake overflows, creating the Jordon River. Barak took us to his brother's place, which was surrounded by gardens with wonderful vegetables and fruits. The climate and soil in this area were perfect for growing. Barak introduced us to his brother, Gideon, and his wife, Tallay. They were younger than Barak and had two children about the ages of Deborah and Noah.

Our children were soon playing with their new friends. Barak left with the promise to bring Pidray is two days. Gideon soon got us situated in our camp, and then he said, "For dinner tonight, we will bring some things from the house, and we will have a good meal together."

Sharmila and Elissa asked if they could help with the preparations, and so they went with Gideon back to the house. The rest of us decided to rest. Even Joel was tired. After a short rest, Joel said to me, "After we get to Tyre, I was wondering: should I try to get a message to Joseph and Jacob's parents? They really need to know that their sons are dead. My parents are dead, thanks to Solomon's work gangs. He worked my father to death, and my mother died soon after. So I do not have to inform anyone about where I am."

"I am sorry that you lost your family, and yours is not an isolated case. As to your question, I am not sure about an answer. My first thought is to wait until we can communicate with Elishama at the academy. He could get in touch with the parents. I think it is best to keep our own situation secret for now."

"I can go along with that; it makes sense."

Mother said, "I am changing the subject. When can we have a funeral service for all four: Joseph, Jacob, Huraya, and Ruth? I would like to have it soon. Could we have it here as soon as Pidray returns?"

"I think we could do that."

Abdi-anati agreed, and our conversation soon became a planning session. It was good that we began to think about this, but our conversation was cut short. Sharmila, Elissa, Gideon and Tallay came each carrying a plate of food. We were sitting at a large table, and now they were putting the food on it and going back for more. What a lovely dinner we had. Gideon was a part-time fisherman. He worked some with Barak, but he also had to spend a majority of his time taking care of the gardens. Gideon told us that most of the traders and people who came for fish also bought garden produce. As you can imagine, our wonderful dinner included fish, many vegetables, bread, honey, cheese, and wine. Mother said to Gideon and Tallay, "This meal is wonderful and your hospitality is gracious. We can never thank you enough."

Gideon said, "We are enriched by your presence. Barak has explained your situation to us, and Barak and I have always been ready to help Abdi-anati and Pidray. We are pleased to help scribes and teachers who try to understand our traditions and our world. We are disturbed by what Solomon is doing to us, and we were glad to hear that you were trying to help

Jeroboam. We also want to send you on your way to Tyre with a donkey-load of fresh vegetables."

Mother said, "In the midst of our personal tragedy, your help is healing, and we thank you very much."

30

AFTER TWO DAYS, BARAK and Arsay brought Pidray to join us. Pidray was looking much better. With so many friends, we actually had a wonderful time, but at the same time we were extremely sad. We had the funeral service in the late afternoon about an hour before dinner.

I started things out by saying that we were having a funeral without the bodies of our loved ones. "This is not what we usually do. In our traditions it is important to bury the body. This was also the case in much earlier traditions from Ugarit. In the ancient story of Danel, his son was murdered. It was necessary for Danel to find the body of his son Aqhat. He finally found his 'fat and bone,' and then they had a funeral. We are not so fortunate. Also in our traditions, it is the criminal or enemy whose body is denied the tomb. He is left out in the wilderness for the vultures to devour. Perhaps some of you recall that in my father's poem, *The Rebel Job*, the rebel is portrayed as innocent; he is not a criminal, and that is why his burial is emphasized. The rebel Job says, 'But as for me, I know that my avenger lives; and a guarantor by [my] grave will stand' (Job 19:25). In our case the criminals got away, and we cannot claim the bodies of our innocent loved ones for burial. It would be too dangerous at this time. Perhaps some day we can claim them. Some of you may recall that according to a few of our stories, after the Philistines hung the bodies of Saul and his sons on the wall of Beth-shan, the men of Jabesh-gilead came and removed them. They cremated them and buried them in Jabesh and fasted for seven days (1 Samuel 31:8–13). Later David buried them in the tomb of Saul's father, Kish (2 Samuel 21:13–14).

"The tomb and the funeral service are important for us, because we call forth the names of those whom we bury during the service at the tomb. Also we seek their blessings, and we remember them by telling their stories. Many times we also call forth the names of our parents and grandparents. Today when we do these things we will have to imagine that we are standing before our tombs as we call forth the names and rehearse their stories. The real fact is that we are gathered here in a most beautiful setting, and as we look beyond to the lake, it is easy to say, '*tov meʾod.*' Yes! Creation is *very good.*

"Before we proceed with our service I would like to read a poem which I have been writing for this occasion, but I am quick to say that it is not really mine. Many voices from the past and present have helped me along the way."

When we part, it is dying a little.
Separation: it is a taste of death—
More work, stress, and yes, awful loneliness.
That is hard language. Can it be that bad?

Yes! Our lives are a series of events;
They make up our story, and they remain.
Each event brings a new reality,
And to part is to miss out on events.
Perhaps the facts can be put in order,
But what of the moods and intentions.
We'll miss actual moments, novel changes,
Like the lost events of those who die young.

When you part from a child or a lover
In urgent times that demand parting,
There is still that awful pain in the throat,
The ache in the nose, and the flow of tears.
It's worse when the other is torn away,
If lost, it's more than dying a little.
Death cannot erase events of the lost,
But it removes the hope of new events.

From these thoughts, a suggestion has surfaced.
Journals are needed for telling our story;
They are crucial for those who survive us.
Those who want to know and tell our story
Can meet grief with the joy of changed moments,
Moments that were creative for the lost.
If there are no journals, we begin now
To save stories of the lost by telling.

At this point we called forth the names: Gad, Jael, Jonathan, and Ruth. Abdi-anati called forth the names of Huraya and her grandparents, and Joel called forth the names of Joseph, Jacob, and their parents. With such a group, it was time to begin our story telling.

Pidray did not feel like speaking, so Sharmila and Abdi-anati came forward to tell Huraya's story. Abdi-anati said, "Huraya was a happy child. She was not only strong and healthy, but she brought light into our lives through her creative moments. It is difficult to believe that she is gone, because those past moments still bring light to these present dark and tragic times. As we look to our future without Huraya and Joseph, we will miss the light of her life, but her past encouragements will come again as gifts from the departed."

Sharmila followed, "I completely agree with what my father has said. I guess I can only add a few examples of how she helped me. As my younger sister, she was a bit of a tease, but she had good judgment. She knew when to tease and when to stop. She knew I had been in love with Naam for a long time, and when other boys were paying too much attention to me, she would start teasing me about my Jerusalem boyfriend. The other boys would soon leave. What a relief. Also I want to say that for quite a few years, I helped father with scribal duties. I could not do all my chores and help mother, so Huraya did not complain, and she helped mother. She took her family responsibilities with a smile. My sister was a wonderful person, and she will always be my ideal; she will be at my side as I make decisions for my future."

Next Joel stepped forward and said, "I want to say a few words about my two closest friends, Joseph and Jacob. I have known Jacob for many years. We were in the academy together, and then we were caretakers for Sheva and Sarah and also for Khety and Tamar. We helped each other in our schoolwork and with our caretaking responsibilities. He was a good person, and he was going to be a wonderful husband for Ruth. He talked about her constantly after he had met her at Naam and Sharmila's wedding. He said at the time that Ruth was too young, but he would wait for her. He will be missed by his parents, the scribal community, and by all who are gathered here.

"I did not know Joseph as well as I knew Jacob, but we worked and lived together as scribes. It was clear from the beginning that Joseph and Huraya were a perfect fit. They complimented each other, and they created an atmosphere of happiness and fun on every occasion. As others have mentioned, they will continue in inspire us, but I will always miss their daily contributions."

Mother and Elissa came forward together. Mother said, "Tragedy has surrounded me once again. This time it is similar to the first time. My mother died as our house burned in Ziklag, and Ruth died in a similar fire in Beth-shan. Ruth was a beautiful young woman. She helped at the academy school; she helped at home; she took care of my grandchildren, and she was thoughtful. She was curious and delighted in uncle Khety's stories. She cannot be replaced, but we can remember her and gain a great deal from our remembrance of her. I know this to be true, because I have gained from my remembrance of my mother. I will need more time to write down some of my fondest memories of Ruth, but I promise before these witnesses to do this for next year's memorial service."

Elissa said, "My sister Ruth and I were very close. We always played together; we studied together; we worked together, and we loved our family. Joel and I will miss her. I will always feel a need for her. I never thought that her beautiful life would end, but I am thankful that we had her even if her time was short."

I began my words with a reference to Samuel. I said, "Samuel should be included in our thoughts today. He gave his life for his support of Jeroboam, who was against Solomon's forced labor atrocities. Joseph, Huraya, Jacob and Ruth gave their lives, because of my involvement in that same cause. In the near future many more will suffer in the north as they stand against Solomon's policies. I am afraid this is only the beginning.

"The great debate between father's rebel Job and the followers of the ancient Job still goes on, and it will never end. According to the ancient Job, suffering and death can be traced to one's sin and a life lived without the fear of God. But the rebel Job voices a hearty *no* to such nonsense. With natural events, such as floods, suffering falls on the innocent and the guilty with equal intensity. But when we look around at the suffering that is caused by our people, it appears that the innocent suffer more than the guilty. This is because in most cases, the guilty are to be identified with the powerful. This is one reason why there is no justice, and it is the reason that the rebel Job stands up for the cause of the powerless. Our loved ones lost their lives; they were innocent and powerless against Solomon's troops. I have to take some blame for involving these fine young people in this fight against Solomon's policies. I did have some indication that my family and friends were of the same mind, but still to lose a young member of your family is a tragic blow. I can only hope that when we relate this story to others they will understand that those in power have slaughtered the innocent."

Shalom!
Shalom to Samuel, Joseph, Huraya, Jacob and Ruth!
Shalom to Abdi-anati, Pidray, Naam, Sharmila, Keziah, Elissa, and Joel!

Shalom to the grandchildren!
Shalom to Barak, Arsay, Gideon, and Tallay!
Shalom to the powerless!
Shalom!

31

ON THE NEXT DAY, I was up early. I did not want to miss a moment of our beautiful surroundings. This day would be a day of rest and packing. Barak and Gideon were already getting some things ready for Abdi-anati and Pidray, because they had nothing but the clothes they were wearing. Gideon also was giving them a donkey, and for all of us, a donkey packed with garden produce. Our plan was to get some sleep in the evening and leave before sunrise. This plan worked out well, and our hosts were up when we left so they could wish us a safe trip.

We spent two days getting to Acco. We were so excited to see the Great Sea that we decided to stay for a day. Our children were delighted to play in the sand and the sea. Abdi-anati and Pidray did find a place to stay, and an old friend of Abdi-anati, who was a scribe, promised Abdi-anati some work. The rest of us took another day and a half to reach Tyre, and when we arrived, we had a great feeling of relief: our trip was over, and we were out of danger from the long arm of Solomon's power.

Mother was overjoyed to see Magon's sister, Elissa, one of her closest friends. Their correspondence through the years had been endless. Elissa was also the inspiration for naming Elissa, my sister. This is going to be confusing. Another confusing element is that Elissa's daughter is Naomi, and Magon's wife is also named Naomi. We will have to clarify our speech. One of the first things mother said to Elissa was: "I always wanted to move to Tyre, and now we are here."

"And I am so glad," Elissa said. " We will have a great time growing old together."

"Yes we will, but before we do that, we will need to find a place to live."

"I think I can help you folks with that. I just received a letter from Magon yesterday. He would like for you folks to live in his uncle's house. It is located right here next to our place, and since I have inherited this place from our father, our uncle gave his place to Magon. Magon said in the letter, 'Keziah, Naam, Sharmila, and their family will need the house, and I will not need it for many years. I will always remember that it was Jonathan who saw to it that a house was built for Naomi and me at the academy.' I know that Magon wants you to be at home in his place. We are here on the mainland in what is called Usu, but it is easy to get to Tyre by boat. It is better to live here and enjoy a garden. Tyre is very crowded these days and actually depends on us for most of its water and wood."

We were all overcome with this generous offer, and mother said, "Magon has always been kind and thoughtful. We will live in his house with thanks, and we will care for it with the understanding that when he needs it, we will find another."

Elissa and her daughter, Naomi, helped us to get settled. Naomi and our Elissa were instant friends. Naomi was three or four years older, but that did not seem to matter. Joel and I cleaned out the spring and repaired a few things. Deborah and Noah even helped. They found some wood and stacked it near the oven.

I could hardly believe that everything seemed to be falling into place in such rapid order.

It is beautiful here in Tyre. The sea is so blue, and I sometimes look west to the horizon; I stare at the sea for long periods of time. The sea is so powerful, and it stretches beyond the limits of our imagination. We call it *hayyam haggadol*, "the great sea." The poets call it *hayyam haggadol mevo' haššemeš*, "the great sea [that harbors] the entrance of the sun." Magon in his psalm on creation describes how "Moon determined the seasons; / Sun knew its entrance" (Psalm 104:19). In other words, the sun knew where to find its entrance into the sea, evening after evening. Our poets refer to Tyre as residing "at the entrances or gateways" to *Yamm* or the sea. They use the plural, "gateways" because of the two ports or harbors at Tyre. The north harbor is called the Sidonian Port and the south harbor is called the Egyptian Port. Ports are named just as the gates of a city; they are named after the city to which the one who exits will travel.

The city of Tyre is on an island just a short distance off shore. Elissa was correct when she said that it is better to live on the mainland in Usu. After a few weeks, I discovered that I went to Tyre about two or three times each week. I crossed from the mainland to the city by boat. After arriving in Tyre, I usually went to both the north harbor and the south harbor. I wanted to see if any new ships had arrived and to find out about their homeports. Also I always asked where they had been and where they were going on this present voyage. I met the sailors who spoke of distant lands and their peoples, and I listened with amazement to their stories. They spoke of Caphtor (Crete), Alashiya (Cyprus), Gebal (Byblos), Egypt, and other places in the north and in the west.

Many of the ships that stop here are sitting low in the water. They have heavy loads, and yet they are here to add to their cargo. Usually they carry mostly raw materials: ingots of copper from Alashiya, tin, a dark blue glass, resin, wine, ebony logs, ivory, figs, fruit, spices, and anchors for ships. After talking with the sailors, I always go to The Tyre Academy. Zadok, who was my father's close friend, is still alive, so I visit with him and other friends. I want to stay in touch and hear the latest news.

Mother, who had wanted to move here on several occasions, enjoys her life in Tyre. She is able to be with Elissa, which is what she had dreamed of doing, and they have wonderful times together. They walk on the beach, and they write poetry.

When I do not go to Tyre, I remain home and tend to my writing. In the future I plan to travel and copy inscriptions along this beautiful coastline. I might go as far north as the ruins of Ugarit and also to the south. I would like to go to Egypt with Khety. These travels will be important for my work, but I also need to translate and work on all the material that I have collected over the years. Also, I want to finish this story of my experiences, and that of my family, as we lived and worked in a community of scribes in Jerusalem during the reigns of David and Solomon. My work on Solomon's reign will be important, because I expect that the royal editors of the chronicles will not give a truthful picture of Solomon's reign. I am certain they will paint an evil portrait of Jeroboam. In addition, after being exiled by Solomon and suffering our losses in Beth-shan, I will be able to keep alive the central arguments in my father's poem, *The Rebel Job*. To tell our story shows beyond a doubt that Solomon's reign is another tragic example of an eternal problem: there is no justice.

32

THERE WILL ALWAYS BE a part of me that would prefer to live in Jerusalem, but usually my Tyre-self wins out. At sea level Tyre is hot and muggy. When it is like that, I long for the light clean air of Jerusalem. Nevertheless, life in Tyre has been wonderful for us. This does not mean we have forgotten the powerless in Israel or the innocents like Ruth and Huraya, lost forever in the flames of Solomon's wrath. But it does mean, we have the time and the setting to absorb the beauty of this earth, motivating us to not only help the powerless but to remind them of two things: true, there is no justice, but the beauty of the earth can nourish the powerless. We all need more than bread.

Our big family news is that Elissa and Joel are now married. Joel spends more time than I do at The Tyre Academy, and Elissa really enjoys working in our garden. Recently I wrote to Khety with this news, and by return message he informed me that everyone in Jerusalem thinks our entire family died at Beth-shan. He noted that sooner or later this mistaken idea would be corrected, but he had no intention of aiding in the process.

Since coming to Tyre, I have found a little more time to be with our children. When Noah and I were walking on the beach one day, we suddenly noticed a sickening and horrible smell. Soon we saw the source. Before us was a mound of crushed sea snails beside a large stone vat. A yellowish liquid in the vat was in the process of rotting and turning black. A man who was working there told us that after it was ready he would add salt and water to the solution. Still later his fellow workmen would use the solution to dye wool. Then I explained to Noah that the wool yarn from this process would be a beautiful dark purple that we call *arganman*. I also mentioned to Noah that the people of Tyre are sometimes called Phoenicians because the word Phoenicia also means purple.

Noah asked, "So what do the people here do with their purple wool?"

"Since it is valuable, they load it on ships and send it to the major cities that surround the great sea. Actually only kings can afford it, and some call it royal purple."

"I would like to see the ships."

"Sometime when I go to Tyre, I will take you with me. The ships and their crews are interesting."

When we got home, the women could still smell the awful snail-odor, and so we cleaned up and changed our clothes. We had a good time around our table during our evening meal. After dinner Elissa came over to our house to visit, and she had a message for me. "I received word today that your father's old friend Zadok is ill, and he wants to see you as soon as possible."

"I will go tomorrow. Zadok and father were friends even before there was a Jerusalem Academy."

Mother said, "They were more than friends, and both of them were shaped by Zadok's teacher and our dear friend, Ahban. After Joab killed Ahban and called him Ahithophel, Zadok came to Tyre as an exile. We have a lot in common with Zadok. You should take him some fresh vegetables from the garden."

Elissa added, "I will send some bread, and if you can manage it, take some of our good spring water. The little amount of water they have in the city has an awful taste."

I left for the city early the next morning. I took Noah with me, and he helped me carry the food and water for Zadok. When I arrived, I went directly to the academy. I found Zadok in his small apartment. He did not look well. First, I set the food and water on his table, and he thanked me again and again. Then I said to him, "What seems to be the matter?"

"I think it is mostly just old age and all the extra baggage that comes with it. My ankles are swollen; when I walk, my legs ache; at night, it is difficult to pee; and my eyes are giving me trouble. But I can manage even with these problems. However, I have recently had a bad cold, and I cough all the time. I wanted to see you, because I know you can help me with a project I am trying to finish before I get too weak. I have ten letters written to Pharaoh from Abi-milku, ruler of Tyre. These letters are copies of letters that were sent to the city, Akhetaten (Amarna), the capital of Egypt, during the time Pharaoh Akh-en-Aton ruled. Written about four hundred years ago, these tablets are important for us to study. We need to understand the problems of the past in order to create a better present and future. Also, I would like to have your comments about a letter that Pharaoh sent to Aziru. The scribes here are not interested in these things, and I do not trust them to take good care of the tablets. The scribes I can trust are all too busy with their own projects to help me with this one."

I said, "I can help you; there is no question. The only thing remaining is to decide on some kind of a schedule."

"We could work on one tablet today, and you could take one with you and bring it back when you finish."

"I really cannot work on one today, but I would be glad to take one home with me. You see my son, Noah, is with me. I promised him a visit to the harbors to see the ships."

"I have a fine and trustworthy student, who can take Noah to see the ships, and we could at least get started on a tablet. My student will be here soon to pick up some work, and I will ask him."

"That would be all right, and in that case I would like to start with the Pharaoh's letter to Aziru."

Zadok's student did arrive and he did agree to take Noah to see the ships. Zadok and I started our work, and it turned out to be an interesting tablet. However, the tablet was a long one, and we soon saw that we could not finish our work on it in one sitting. So I suggested that I take it home and return in two days. About that time Noah returned. He was excited and said that the ships were wonderful. Saying goodbye, I told Zadok to take care and rest so he could get over his cold.

All the way home, Noah was talking excitedly about the ships. He said, "We finished our tour at the Egyptian Port. A scribe was there from The Tyre Academy, and he was going to Egypt on one of the ships. I want to see it too. So when Khety comes to visit, Khety, you, and I should go by ship to Egypt. That would be wonderful."

"It would be, and I must say that you have come up with an interesting plan. Who knows? We just might do something like that."

Around the dinner table, we reported to the rest of the family about our day in Tyre. Noah repeated his plan for an Egyptian trip, and I told them about the tablets. Mother remembered how I was determined to go to Beth-shan with father and Khety years ago, and she said that if Zadok did not feel better in two days, I should bring him home with me. I said, "I will do just that."

The next morning, I started working on the tablet before breakfast. The tablet was a message from Pharaoh to Aziru. Pharaoh was angry with Aziru for claiming to be a faithful servant, when in fact, he was working for the enemy. So Pharaoh prepared a list of his enemies that Aziru was supposed to send to Egypt. This tablet is important to the story of Aziru, who really was not a faithful servant. However something else caught my attention. As a scribe, I am always interested in who wrote the text for Pharaoh. Since it is written in Babylonian, the international language of diplomacy, did Pharaoh have a scribe from Babylon? My answer was no. It seems clear to me that this letter was written by an Egyptian scribe. In fact, I think it was first written in Egyptian and then translated into a localized Babylonian. Even so, the original Egyptian shines through the translation.

When I was translating Egyptian stories, I noticed that in sections of the narrative that contained dialogue, the words were sometimes attributed to the speaker at the beginning of his speech and again at the end. So I was not surprised to see this kind of double attribution in Pharaoh's letter. Here are the first sixlines of my translation, and I have underlined the Egyptian style of double attribution:

> To Aziru, the ruler of Amurru, say:
> Thus says the King, your Lord:
> "Thus says, the ruler of Gubla, whose brother threw him out at the gate.
> He said to you, 'Thus [I] say, "Take me, and bring me into my city. There is much silver, and I will give [it] to you.
> Also there is a great amount of everything, but [it] is not with me."'
> In this manner he spoke to you."

This letter is the work of an Egyptian scribe, and that is important to know.

33

THE LAST TWO DAYS have passed quickly, and so I must return to Tyre today and check in on Zadok. I will also take him more of our wonderful spring water.

When I arrived at Zadok's apartment, he invited me in. He did not look well, and I said to him, "I'm sure you remember my mother, Keziah. She told me to bring you to our place if you were still sick. I will help you gather up the tablets and anything else you might need, and we can continue our work at our home. Also, you can enjoy some good meals and perhaps get to feeling better."

Zadok said, "I did not want to bother you folks, but I am beginning to think I should accept your offer. I can be ready soon."

"That's great. After we gather your things, I will go downstairs to your library and take a look at a couple of items. I will be back soon, and we will be home for lunch."

When I returned, Zadok was ready, and we left at once. He had wrapped the tablets in a wool cloth and put them in a leather bag. I carried the bag, and he carried a few extra clothes. Zadok did not feel well, but he did enjoy being outside. The short boat trip to Usu was invigorating. When we arrived at the house, he was happy to see mother after so many years. She welcomed him as did our Elissa, and Zadok could hardly believe that Elissa had grown from a little girl to a beautiful woman who was now carrying her first child. Then he met Joel and Sharmila. We all sat down for some lunch, and Zadok ate well. The conversation consisted of Zadok's many questions and our answers. We brought him up-to-date on Jerusalem, the academy, father's death, and our flight to Beth-shan. Zadok told Sharmila that he remembered her father and his visits to The Tyre Academy. After lunch he was tired, so I took him to an extra room where he could rest. He rested for most of the afternoon, and while he was resting, Joel and I looked at some of the tablets. When Sharmila brought Zadok out of the house, we were still sitting outside reading tablets. I thanked Sharmila and said to Zadok, "Are you feeling better?"

"Yes, and I feel rested."

"That is good to hear. Joel and I have been looking at the tablets, and we think they tell us a lot about life in Tyre and Usu in the time of Pharaoh Akh-en-Aton. Reading these tablets is informative, but it is also an emotional experience. When Tyre's ruler, Abi-milku, pleads for help from Akh-en-Aton, I can imagine the tears in his eyes."

Zadok said, "When I read them, I have similar experiences. I have read them many times, so it is good that you have started. It is really a great gift that we have these words from the past. What I would like to do in the next few days, with your help, is to come up with a summary of what these tablets tell us about Abi-milku's experience. In addition, we need to emphasize what we can learn from him. To understand this past allows us to deal with our present and future. I want to make a copy of our work to give to King Hiram."

"This is an important project. We should discuss each tablet, and Joel can take some notes. On the basis of my memory and his notes, I will write the summary. We can also discuss the summary, and you will have to translate it into the language of Tyre."

Zadok said, "You are like your father; he was always able to come up with a plan. His plans were usually helpful, and your plan delegates the work and makes sense."

"I will spend tomorrow reading these texts with care, and the next day we can discuss them. Joel, you can record some of what we conclude. Zadok, we want you to rest, but I may disturb you from time to time with a question."

Just as I finished, Mother called us to dinner. The dinner was very good, and Elissa and Naomi from next door joined us. As usual Elissa brought something to supplement our table. This time she brought fresh bread, new honey, and tasty cheese. She also had received a message from Magon and wanted to share the news. She said, "Magon says that things are going well at the academy. He thinks Solomon is not interfering as much, because he knows his soldiers went too far when they burned Abdi-anati's house in Beth-shan. In any case, Elishama is doing well, and Khety has large classes and hopes to visit Tyre in the near future."

Zadok said, "I would like to meet Khety, but I would like for you to ask your brother to visit us. Magon was always helpful. Actually we could use his help with the project we are doing now."

I said, "It is good to hear about things in Jerusalem, and I do hope our friends come to sit at this table. Our table talk keeps us alive."

Mother said, "I could not agree more, and this evening proves the point. We are ten souls with bodies that relish and need this good food and minds that thirst for lively conversation."

Sharmila said, "How true, and I noticed that Noah and Deborah suddenly had a twinkle in their eyes with the mention of uncle Khety making a visit."

I spent the next day reading the ten texts. I decided that it was not going to be difficult to write about the contents. Important things were presented in the texts, but there was also a lot of repetition. Here is my report:

THE LETTERS OF ABI-MILKU OF TYRE TO KING AKH-EN-ATON (1–10)

In these letters the addressee (or the King) is always praised in the address and in the prostration formula ("Seven times seven I fall at the feet of the King, my Lord"). Some of the longer letters, like tablet 2, praise the Egyptian king throughout the text. In the address of tablet 2, we have: "To the King, my Lord, my Gods, my Sun." There are four other tablets that use the plural "my Gods." This is interesting and in tablet 6 there is both the singular and the plural: "To the King, my Sun, my God, my Gods." I am not sure I understand this, but this is what is written. In tablet 2, Abi-milku praises the King for many things: As the Sun he shines over the land and the people. He is the one who gives life by his sweet breath, and establishes peace in the land by his strong arm. Because of all of this, Abi-milku promises to prepare for the coming of the King's army. The army will need food and other supplies. He also takes on the task of guarding Tyre, which he calls the city of the King (this task of guarding is also stressed in tablets 1, 4, 5, 8, and 10).

Tablet 2, lines 45–51, presents a perfect description of the origin of the doctrine of retribution. The preceding lines describe the obedient vassal servant and how the King or Pharaoh blesses him. Then we have the following lines:

> ù la-a iš-te-mi a-ma-ta5 LUGAL be-lí-šu
> hal-qá-at URU-[š]u ha-li-iq É- šu
> ia-nu šu-um-šu i-na gáb-bi

KUR-ti i-na da-ri-ti a-mur
ÌR-da ša iš-me a-na (a-na) be-li-šu
šul-mu URU- šu šul-mu É-šu
šu-um-šu a-na da-ri-ti

If he does not listen to the word of the King, his Lord,
lost is his city; perished is his house,
and his name will not exist in all
the land ever again. Behold
the servant who listens to his Lord.
Healthy is his city; healthy is his house.
His name exists forever.

The tablets detail a complaint that Zimredda, the King of Sidon, is hostile to Abi-milku, and that means Abi-milku cannot get fresh water from Usu. In fact, the phrase, "I need wood and water" becomes a constant chant in these tablets (tablets 1 and 2). In tablet 3, Abi-milku promises to send the King a hundred units of glass and then expands his usual request to the King. He says, "Give Usu to his servant for water." Later he adds, "for wood, for straw, for clay." Apparently the scribes needed more clay in order to write more messages.

In tablet 4, the complaint against Zimredda is expanded. Now he has seized Usu, and Tyre is without water or wood. In addition, the citizens of Tyre have no place to bury their dead. Also, there is a real danger that Zimredda and his fellow rebels will capture Tyre. Here is a call for help. This plea for help is continued in tablet 5. Abi-milku pleads to the King to give him Usu that he may live and drink water. Also, his people are crying for wood. Tablets 6–9 continue to plead for help, and in tablet 10, it is made clear that wood, water, straw, supplies, and burial plots are needed for the living. For the gift of life, Abi-milku will guard the King's ships in his harbors.

One of the major insights of these tablets is that the King of Tyre must control Usu. Therefore, in our day, it is prudent for the King of Tyre to control a buffer strip of land to the east of his port cities starting in the south at Acco and running north past Tyre to Sidon. Therefore, the cities that Solomon gave to Hiram may not be important as cities go, but the strip of land that came with the cities is just what Hiram needs for defense, now and in the future.

With this summary, we will have a good discussion tomorrow.

34

By MORNING, ZADOK WAS well rested and feeling much better. After breakfast Joel, Zadok, and I went outside to the table that we keep under one of our shade trees. I read my summary of the ten tablets to them, and they made comments and asked questions. I expanded some of my points, and we had a productive session.

Zadok's first point concerned my question about the meaning of "my Gods" in the address of these tablets and especially the address in tablet 6: "To the King, my Sun, my God, my Gods." He said, "You must remember that in this case the King or Pharaoh was Akh-en-Aton. He ruled about four hundred years ago, and we now know that he revolted against some of the old Egyptian gods. He eliminated some gods from their functions in the cult—including Osiris from mortuary rituals. Akh-en-Aton worshiped Aton, his God and Sun, and the people worshiped Akh-en-Aton, their God and Sun. When the scribes addressed Akh-en-Aton in these letters they said, 'To the King, my Sun, my God, my Gods,' and 'my Gods' refers to Akh-en-Aton and Aton. When Khety comes to visit you, we should ask him about this subject."

"Your response makes sense to me, and I agree that we should ask Khety about Akh-en-Aton's impact on Egypt's later developments."

Joel said, "I recall from Khety's classes that Akh-en-Aton's religious reforms did not last, but his reformation was a broad program that brought about changes in language, art, and personal relationships."

"Right you are, and I remember Khety's suggestion that some of the women from Mitanni, who were in Pharaoh's harem, spoke out and helped to increase the rights and freedom of women. When Sharmila and I were married, he made that point after reading *The Enchanted Prince* at our party."

Zadok said, "Here we sit under a shade tree in Usu, and in your summary you stressed how important Usu is to Tyre. Usu gave the gift of life to Tyre by providing it with a source of fresh water. This is perhaps the most important point in your summary for my project. I want to show that King Hiram of Tyre has cleverly out maneuvered Solomon. Indeed, when he told

Solomon he was not pleased with the twenty cities that Solomon gave him, he did not let on to Solomon that, even though the cities were not pleasing, the buffer zone that came with them to the east of his port cities was priceless. King Hiram has learned from the past, and these texts show without a doubt that Abi-milku found himself in dire straits, because he did not have such a buffer zone. He could not even keep Usu under his control. In my report to King Hiram, I will stress this point above all others. I will not mention your discussion about the origin of the doctrine of retribution, because as we know, kings do not like to hear criticism of their views on justice."

"I understand. There is no need to antagonize the king at this time."

Joel responded, "I also understand, but I want to add that this example of the doctrine of retribution is really clear. I think we all know how this doctrine developed, but it is nice to see it spelled out syllable after syllable. Your translation, 'If he does not listen to the word of the King' is probably the best and most neutral way to do it. Though I remember Magon telling us that 'listen' in such contexts usually can be translated 'obey.' Also, I take it that 'his house' refers to his royal line or dynasty, which will perish if he, or in this case Abi-milku, does not obey the word of the Pharaoh?"

"That is correct, and I find this interesting. Abi-milku and other such vassal rulers have always known that their continued relationship with the great King or Pharaoh was dependent upon their obedience. In other words, it was conditional: if you do not obey your house will perish. But David in his last years, and now Solomon, believe their covenant with their great King, or Yahweh, is not conditional but eternal. This brings about a real problem for Solomon or any other king who claims that his house is eternal, even with the presence of disobedient heirs. Why? Because the doctrine of retribution, which they all endorse, as seen here in tablet 2 and in *The Ancient Story of Job*, says, 'Listen/obey and all will be well; disobey and all will be lost.' Solomon's position on his eternal house stands over and against his belief in the doctrine of retribution. He is a living contradiction."

Zadok said, "I think you are right. Also, Solomon's burning of your sister and Sharmila's sister is not an example of the doctrine of retribution. Those innocent ones were murdered. I notice that in tablet 2, if the vassal king is obedient, his city and his house will be healthy, and his name will exist forever. Here the Babylonian word, which you have translated as 'healthy,' is our word *shalom*, which also means 'to be sound' and 'to be complete.' I can remember your father talking about this business of retribution. He maintained that it was a poor excuse for justice. Of course, he never tired of insisting that there is no justice. This was also the theme in his poem, *The Rebel Job,* as you well know, and now you have experienced this fact in your life."

"Yes, we have experienced it. One of the difficulties in our work is dealing with such things. The doctrine of retribution makes some sense when you are dealing with the relationship between two kings, but it cannot be extended as an explanation of suffering in general. Which brings up an unrelated question: does King Hiram know Solomon's crime against us?"

Zadok answered, "I do not think he knows about that, but he does know that you taught in The Jerusalem Academy, and that I was a close friend of your father. Of course, you have told me that Solomon thinks you are dead, and therefore, it is best just to leave things as they are."

"I agree. It is interesting to consider what it means to be an exile. In many ways we are free, and we do have a good life here in Usu. But we are not free to go back to Jerusalem or to charge Solomon with his crimes."

Just then Sharmila, mother, and Elissa came out and joined us, bringing fresh and cool water from our spring. They asked about our discussion, and we emphasized the importance of Usu and the spring water it supplies for those living in Tyre.

Sharmila was looking at one of the tablets, which was on the table. She asked, "Are scribes still writing on clay tablets and using Babylonian and writing like this?"

"Yes," answered Zadok, "but it is mostly in the east. The scribes at Ugarit developed an alphabet, which simplified things, but they still used cuneiform signs and wrote on clay. They used thirty letters instead of the hundreds of signs used in Babylonian. This alphabet was simplified again by our coastal cities. In the present language of Tyre and of Jerusalem, we use only twenty-two letters. You might ask, why? The answer is because we do not distinguish as many sounds as they did at Ugarit. We allowed similar sounds to blend together. We only needed twenty-two letters because we only had twenty-two sounds to express. However, we had to learn from Crete and other western islands to use a linear alphabet before we could write on parchment and papyrus with ink. As you well know, our alphabets are made with lines."

I said, "I would only add that the Egyptian scribes also helped us to move to a linear alphabet. I say this because the Egyptians found out that instead of drawing a complete and intricate hieroglyph they could just abbreviate the picture with three or four strokes or lines. I should also say that the Egyptians did have an alphabet, but they never took advantage of it; they allowed it to stand in the midst of their complicated system of hieroglyphs."

Mother said, "My life completely changed when I learned our alphabet. The alphabet was a great discovery. No, it was more than a discovery; it was means of gaining freedom and experiencing the many worlds both past and present."

After this conversation, we noticed that we had not even thought about lunch, and it was almost time for dinner.

35

Mother loved her new life in Tyre, or actually, in Usu. She spent at least half of each day with Magon's sister Elissa, and her daughter, Naomi, was with my sister Elissa just as much, or perhaps more. This does not mean that mother did not miss Jerusalem and her many friends. When my sister Elissa had her baby girl, mother was overjoyed. She also loved my children, Deborah and Noah, but for her, Elissa's baby was a special blessing in light of the loss of Ruth. She often said that she wanted to live long enough to see her third grandchild grow to be a mature woman. She may do that. She always contributes to our work, our conversations, and to every aspect of our lives. The other day when she was talking about the importance of the alphabet, I was reminded of how she gets right to the heart of any discussion in a clear and insightful manner.

As the years passed, we continued to enjoy our life in Usu and Tyre. I did get to travel to many of the coastal cities, and Khety visited us twice. Khety's visits kept me up to date on the progress of The Jerusalem Academy and also on Solomon's activities. We also visited Sharmila's parents in Acco. They were happy in their new home, and there was plenty of work for an experienced scribe like Abdi-anati. They were still in contact with friends in Beth-shan, so they kept us up-to-date on how northern Israel was doing. Solomon's policies were still causing a great deal of suffering.

On one of Khety's visits he invited me to go with him to Egypt. I accepted his invitation eagerly, because among other things, I was anxious to see Jeroboam. This was an important journey for me. When Noah was young, he said that we should go to Egypt with Khety. I am sorry that we this did not happen. However, Noah did not wait. He has already gone to Egypt during his training as a sailor. We traveled by land, and our trip south was hot. We were glad to get to *Djanet* (Hebrew *Zoan* and Greek *Tanis*) where we could rest in the shade. However, we soon found out that Pharaoh Shishak had moved his capital to Bubastis, which meant we had to move on. We went to his capital, because we understood that Pharaoh

Shishak had welcomed Jeroboam to Egypt, and that Jeroboam had married Pharaoh Shishak's sister-in-law. This was not an easy trip for us, but Khety knew his way around. Bubastis was located along the banks of the great river that the Egyptians call "*Iteru*" (the Nile). I say "banks" because it seemed as if the *Iteru* was everywhere. with many islands and canals. It was beautiful, but you really did need a boat to get around. We found Jeroboam in Bubastis, where he lived in a beautiful house that was part of the palace complex. Jeroboam and I were not close friends, but I had talked with him on several occasions when I was with Samuel. Khety and Jeroboam had never met, but they knew about each other. He was glad to see us. His first question was, "What can you tell me about Samuel?"

I told him the entire story of our meeting with Samuel and Rachel to help them make plans for their escape. I described Samuel's arrest, and then I said, "We never saw Samuel again. Rachel is living with her folks, and she helps her father at the academy."

Jeroboam was visibly shaken with this news; he could not speak for several moments. With halting speech, he said, "I am so sorry to hear this. Samuel was my best friend from early childhood. I regret that my problems became his problems and led to his death, and I know that others have given their lives as well. I just hope their lives have not been lost for nothing."

"You mentioned others, and I must tell you that my family and I also had to escape from Jerusalem. We went to Beth-shan to stay with my wife's parents. Her father, Abdi-anati, was a scribe there. We thought that we were safe, but we were mistaken. We received a message from Elishama, who is now the head of the academy. He said that a group of Solomon's soldiers were on their way to Beth-shan, and they were looking for me. We managed to leave Beth-shan before the soldiers arrived, thanks to Abdi-anati and his friends. However, the soldiers set fire to Abdi-anati's house, believing I was there, and my sister and Abdi-anati's youngest daughter were burned to death along with others. There are many others, as you have mentioned, who have suffered such losses; we are not the only ones."

"I am sorry to hear this story, and it is not unlike other reports that have reached me. Solomon is making things worse every day. How is the rest of your family?"

"My mother, my wife, my children, and my sister are doing quite well. We live in Usu, and I am doing some work at The Tyre Academy. I keep in touch with my friends at The Jerusalem Academy. Khety has been bringing me up-to-date with more news of the academy on this trip."

"Do you think you will ever go back to Jerusalem?"

"I do not know, but I do know that I will not go back until Solomon is dead."

"That is my situation as well. My friends say that as soon as Solomon dies, they will send word. They expect me to return to Shechem and help them decide what to do."

Khety asked, "Is there any possibility that Israel would still remain united with the House of David or Judah after the death of Solomon?"

Jeroboam answered, "I doubt it, because I think Solomon's successor will probably make things worse for Israel. In any case, I am glad to know I have a friend at Tyre. Israel will need friends in many places if it intends to take a stand against Judah."

I said, "If the people want you to lead them in a stand against Judah, will you do it."

"I would have to do it. It will not be an easy task to organize Israel to defend itself and to provide for the people. Their needs are great. For too long our life—by which I mean our economic, spiritual, and cultic life—has been centered on the House of David in Jerusalem. All of this has to change. Also, we must revitalize the Shechem scribal school and turn it into an academy. I was hoping that Samuel would be able to help us with this, but he will not be around. Perhaps Elishama or you could help us do this?"

"I am sure that both of us could help you with finding personnel, even if we did not participate in the school. But I do want to make a point: what we do in any good academy must be greater than any local political problem. By this, I do not mean that local political problems are not important. They are important, but they should not be allowed to destroy the freedom of an academy to search for wisdom from every quarter and every land."

"Now I know why Samuel was so taken with you."

I continued, changing the subject, "How do you like living here with the *Iteru* creating islands and canals? There seems to be water everywhere I look."

"It is a lively and interesting place, but I prefer the dry country up the river. I have been up river to *Waset,* as the Egyptians call it. Another Egyptian name for *Waset,* is *Niwet-'Amon,* meaning "the City of Amon." In Israel we pronounce this place name, *No'-'Amon* (later Greek Thebes). I think you would like it there, and there is much to see. It is a long trip, but not so bad by boat."

Khety said, "I plan to take Naam to *Niwet-'Amon,* and I will use the opportunity to check on some of my relatives and friends."

Jeroboam served us a wonderful dinner, and it was interesting to meet his wife and his young son, Abijah. We stayed overnight with Jeroboam, and we promised to stay in touch with him.

We went to *Waset* to see the great monuments of Thut-mose and the palace of Amen-hotep. This was a long trip, but quite easy by boat. The entire complex at and around *Waset* was tremendous, almost unimaginable in beauty and size. What was also of great interest to Khety and to me was the long list of cities that Thut-mose conquered during his military campaigns. Of particular interest to me was the list in the great temple of Amon. Here it shows that Thut-mose went to *mtn* or Mitanni, and in the list of Amen-hotep and in the list of Seti, we saw the Egyptian form *nhrn* or Naharin. As I learned from working on *The Enchanted Prince*, the Egyptians had been in the northern part of the Mitanni Kingdom or Naharin and even in the northeastern part near ancient Nuzi. In the list of Seti, I also saw Usu, my present hometown. This was extremely important to me. I like knowing that the inscriptions refer to a past that was actually real.

We took a boat down-river and were able to board a ship going to Tyre. The trip by sea was pleasant, and we were in sight of land most of the way. This route gave me the opportunity to experience the same identical voyage that Wen-Amon took years ago and described for us in *The Report of Wen-Amon*.

After arriving at Tyre, we went to Usu and home. Everyone was glad to see us, and they all had a good time talking with Khety around our table. Khety left for Jerusalem the next day because he was anxious to get home and give Tamar the news about his family and friends in Egypt. Also, I was excited about discussing with my family the things I saw in Egypt and the details of my conversation with Jeroboam. I asked Khety to tell Elishama about Jeroboam and especially about his remarks concerning the school at Shechem. After explaining to mother and Sharmila about Jeroboam's hopes for a school in Shechem, I said, "If we cannot go back to The Jerusalem Academy, we just might end up in Shechem. They both agreed that Shechem might be an interesting and important place to work.

36

THE NEXT FEW YEARS were good years. Mother enjoyed her grandchildren, her friends, and our garden. By the time she was eighty, she was slowing down in terms of her garden work, but she was very alert and still wrote poetry daily. She continued to be an amazing and beautiful woman. Now into her eighty-third year, she spent most of her time putting her writings in order, and then one day, without warning, she died. It is hard to believe that it has now been twenty years since my father died at the age of seventy. We buried mother in the family tomb of her friend, Elissa. Elissa said that they wanted to be buried together. There was room, because Magon, who had died earlier, was buried in Jerusalem. Elissa also said that she would not last much longer. Her daughter, Naomi, takes care of her mother and remains very close to my sister, Elissa. Sharmila also spends time with the two of them. When mother died, I was sixty-three. Needless to say, we all miss mother. She was such a vital presence, and she was so central to our family. She will always be remembered as one who helped others and as a scholar who liberated minority opinions from our past—these opinions created the context for adventure and a more meaningful future. I recently found one of her short essays on a minority opinion that did not make it into her book. She began by quoting one of our old traditions. I will give the entire essay here:

TREES

"When you besiege a city for many days, making war against it in order to capture it, you shall not destroy its trees by swinging an axe against them. Yes, from them you may eat, but you shall not cut them down. Are the trees of the field human beings, able to flee from your presence to that of the besieged? Only trees of which you know that they are not food trees, you may destroy, and you may cut them down, and you may build siegeworks with them against the city that is waging war with you until its defeat" (Deut 20:19–20).

Trees that produce food, usually fruit trees, are not to be destroyed as if they were humans and, therefore, your enemies. I do not know when our ancestors came up with this idea, but it is a good one. We should value trees that produce food. Warfare is bad enough without killing trees. I do not think we have ever paid much attention to this commandment, but we should observe it. It is interesting to me that the first humans, who were told not to eat of the tree of the knowledge of good and evil, ate of the forbidden tree and accepted the penalty of mortality in order to gain all knowledge. This was a fortunate act, because now in this later commandment we need knowledge: you can only destroy trees that you know are not food trees.

Mother cared for our plants and trees. I can imagine that as she cared for them she thought about this old commandment that seems to be unique among our various traditions. She would be the first to say that our ancestors may have paid no attention to this commandment, but she would also stress that to be human is to care for the powerless and that includes plants and trees.

About once every other month, Sharmila and I go to Acco to visit her parents. They are getting old, but they are still in good health. They recently heard some good news from Beth-shan. Some of their friends in Beth-shan did recover the bodies of Ruth and Huraya and they were buried. Some day we will visit their graves.

When we are home, both of us do a lot of writing, and I should say that Sharmila is producing the final copy of this work. I give her a chapter, and she soon corrects it and gives it back in her beautiful hand. Our children, Deborah and Noah, are both grown and gone. I was not surprised when Noah announced that he wanted to be a sailor. He is having a good life and has been to many places. King Hiram needs good sailors, and now that he does some shipping with Solomon, he needs sailors, who know the languages of Canaan and Tyre and can read and write. Deborah lives in Acco near her grandparents. She married a young scribe, who works for Abdi-anati, and she can help her grandparents whenever they need extra help.

Joel still goes to Tyre and does some work at the academy, but I actually get more accomplished here at home. However, Sharmila and I decided to go on a trip along our northern coast. Joel went with us, and he brought along one of his friends from The Tyre Academy. His name is Danel, and he grew up near ancient Ugarit in Ramitha (Latakia), which is just a little south of Ugarit. Not many people in Ramitha still remember the name of the city ruins to their north. After all, the Sea Peoples destroyed Ugarit about two hundred years ago. But a few fishermen still remember their families telling stories about Ugarit and its harbor and small village, Mahadu (Minet el-Beida). After the destruction of Ugarit and Mahadu, the harbor at Ramitha became the harbor of choice.

Once again, we put a few things on two donkeys and traveled at a slow pace. In a conversation with Danel, I told him that my father had a good friend years ago in The Jerusalem Academy with the name Danel. Danel replied that at The Tyre Academy it was a popular name, because Danel was an ancient hero from Ugaritic stories. I told him that in our old traditions, we listed Danel along with our ancient Job and Noah; they were considered righteous men. We had some good conversations on our trip, and we ate locally grown food as we moved from town to town. We stopped at Sidon, Biruta (Beirut), and Gubla (Byblos). In all of these ports, we always took the time to look at the ships. Before we left on this trip, Noah told us to do this. So we became acquainted with all kinds of ships and their equipment. Going on north from Gubla we just enjoyed the beauty of the sea.

As we approached Ramitha we beheld a beautiful sight: a round and well-protected blue bay with a shoreline of white sand framing it. To the east was a range of hills that protected the city from the hot desert winds. The foothills to the east were a perfect place for vineyards, and Danel told us that the wine in his hometown was better than any in Tyre. We could also see the harbor facilities, and we watched several ships being loaded. The pace of our journey suddenly picked up, because Danel was anxious to see his family. Danel's father was a fisherman, and he also worked at the harbor loading and unloading ships. He came from a long line of fisher-men, and he was one of the few among the fishermen, who knew about ancient Ugarit and Mahadu.

We arrived in Ramitha in the afternoon, so we had time to enjoy the beach, the water, and the shade before dinner. The dinner, prepared by Danel's mother and extended family, was a welcomed treat. There was plenty of good local wine to go with the lamb and delicious vegetables. Sharmila helped in the preparations, so she could learn how they prepared their foods. The olives were very good, and Sharmila asked for and received detailed instruction for curing them. First, she was told to put the green olives on a reed mat and crack them with a wooden mallet. Second, put the cracked olives in a large pot and fill it with water. Next, add salt to the mixture. When Sharmila asked how much salt do you use? They answered, "You put a fresh egg in the water, and you add salt until the egg floats. After about two weeks, you drain off the salt water, rinse the olives, and add fresh water for storage."

We had a wonderful time during and after the dinner. We talked with Danel's father, Kalbu, concerning Ugarit, and he offered to take us there the next day. Later that evening when Sharmila was writing in her journal, she included the instructions for the curing of Ramitha olives.

The next morning we had a delightful breakfast, and then we packed a lunch. We left early for our walk to the ruins of Mahadu and Ugarit. This was a pleasant walk, and Kalbu explained to us the importance of moving the port for this area to Ramitha after the destruction of Ugarit and its port, Mahadu. As we approached the old port city, Kalbu pointed out the round and sheltered bay at Mahadu. He said, "This port is as good as ours at Ramitha, but a port or harbor needs a city. In this case, both city and harbor were destroyed. When the harbor for this area was established at Ramitha, both city and harbor facilities grew in size and efficiency. Some equipment for the ships was even moved from Mahadu to Ramitha."

I asked, "What kind of equipment?"

"Stone anchors, fishing gear, and even some timbers and planks. This is what my father told me, and it was repeated again and again in some of our rituals. It is important for our sailors that Baal defeated Yamm, or the sea. Our anchors save lives when we need to ride out a storm, and we see to it that Baal blesses our anchors. They are beautiful to us, and the anchors that came from Mahadu years ago have been blessed through the ages. In fact, one of the anchors that has a prominent place at our alter for Baal is inscribed with the Egyptian hieroglyph for *nefer*, meaning "beautiful.""

At once, I drew the *nefer* glyph on the sandy path on which we were walking. It consisted of a heart plus a windpipe, and I asked Kalbu if this is the glyph that is carved on the anchor. He answered, "That is it. You must know Egyptian."

"I know some, because I had a good teacher."

It was only a short distance from the harbor up to the ancient city of Ugarit. After the Sea Peoples destroyed it, it was not rebuilt, and some walls could still be seen in spite of the rubble, the weeds, and the brush. The most impressive thing to me was the size of the city. It was very big, and it would take many days to look carefully at all of it. I noticed that Joel and Sharmila stood still, completely amazed. Sharmila said, "I wonder if Jerusalem will look like this some day to visitors from later times."

As we walked west on our way back to the port, I noticed a piece of clay lying among some broken pottery. I picked it up; it looked like the top part of a tablet. I brushed off some dirt and read the beginning of the text written in Babylonian: "Thus says the King of Carchemish to the King of Ugarit, saying . . ." I called to the others and said, "Look what I found. Here we have the first three lines of a letter. It is from the King of Carchemish to the King of Ugarit. I would like to have the entire letter, but even these opening lines are important. There is no doubt that we are standing on the ancient site of the city of Ugarit."

Kalbu said, "I am glad that you found this broken letter. I usually believe the traditions that have been passed down to us from our ancestors, especially concerning places, but still it is nice to have written evidence that the traditions are correct."

"I certainly agree with you that our oral traditions usually have places and names right. Sometimes they add a lot of things that our heroes do, but it is difficult to add names and invent places. That is especially true for places like Ugarit. It was only a few days ago that I was reading the letters of Abi-milku of Tyre to King Akh-en-Aton of Egypt, and Akh-en-Aton wanted some information about Canaan. So Abi-milku told him, among other things, that fire had destroyed half of the house of the king, or the palace, at Ugarit. It is quite clear that Ugarit was an important city, and its port was a primary shipping center. If we had the time to clear and expose some of these old buildings, I am certain that we could find many tablets."

Sharmila said, "I would like to go down to the harbor and put my feet in the water. It would also be a nice place for us to eat our lunch."

We had a pleasant time as we ate our lunch. I sat there imagining the harbor full of ships. Change is always with us, but I sometimes long for increased stability. The destruction of Ugarit was too complete. Just a few buildings left standing would have allowed us to imagine what it was like.

We also had a nice walk back to Ramitha. What a day to remember.

37

OUR STAY AT RAMITHA was good for us. We had good food and wonderful table talk. But Joel and Danel needed to get back to Tyre, and Elissa was probably expecting us by now. We essentially retraced our steps, and we never tired of viewing the beautiful coast.

When we got home Elissa was relieved to see us home safely. The next day Joel went to Tyre and brought home a couple of letters for me—a letter from Khety and a letter from Jeroboam.

Khety's letter contained shocking news. He wrote, "The academy is doing fine and keeping its distance from recent political events including the death of Solomon."

Setting the letter aside, I called out to Sharmila, Elissa, and Joel. They came running, and I told them, "I stopped reading Khety's letter after he mentioned the death of Solomon, and I called you. Yes, Solomon is dead!"

We were all stunned. We were glad, but we were also a bit uneasy to think that death brings such joy. However, in this case thousands have suffered during his reign, and this fact alone makes joy the immediate response.

Sharmila said, "I cannot wait for the rest of the letter. Please read on."

Khety writes, "The death of Solomon is a major political event, because his son, Rehoboam, will succeed him, and Rehoboam is not as wise as his father. Also, we hear that the elders in the north, or to be exact in Shechem, have little interest in continuing with the line of David after what they have suffered under Solomon. We just heard the other day that these elders have written to Jeroboam in Egypt. They want him to return and help them in this time of crises, and as you and I know from our wonderful trip to Egypt and talking with him, he is quite willing. Tamar and I are doing well as is Rachel, who still helps her father with his work. I do not think Elishama could handle his job without her. For now, one of Magon's students is taking over his Babylonian courses. We do miss Magon, and know it well, we miss all of you."

"That is a wonderful letter," Sharmila said, "and I miss them as well."

I turned to Jeroboam's letter and read it for all to hear. After a usual salutation Jeroboam said: "You have probably heard that Solomon is dead. My friends in Shechem sent word to me, and I arrived in Shechem yesterday. The elders have asked Rehoboam to lighten the heavy yoke of hard service that Solomon placed upon them. They will meet with Rehoboam again in three days to hear his answer. I will be at that meeting. Also, I am hoping that you will consider coming to Shechem. We will need help in building a stronger scribal school, and I know your help would be the best. You could help us for a short time, or for the all days that are left for you. I will write to you again after the next meeting with Rehoboam. Send an answer soon."

"So the question is: should I help Jeroboam? It is obvious that an answer is not possible until we hear again from him. I suspect that the Shechem assembly will declare him king of Israel. If this happens, I think we should at least consider going to Shechem."

Joel said, "If you decide to go to Shechem, you could make an important contribution to the Shechem School, but Elissa and I want to stay here. I have work to do in Tyre, and this will give you a home base when you want to visit from time to time. We will want to see you, and you will want to check in with Deborah and Noah. Also Sharmila will want to see her parents in Acco."

Sharmila answered, "Joel, your plan is thoughtful and makes a lot of sense. I will want to visit my parents, and there is no doubt, the children are here to stay."

We did not have to wait long for Jeroboam's next letter; it was informative, clear, and inviting. He explained that he and the elders had met Rehoboam in Shechem. He went on to say that this meeting featured a strange and frantic Rehoboam. He must have been out of his mind because he said that he would increase the burden that Solomon had placed upon the people of the north. The elders made a quick decision; Israel would not accept Rehoboam as their king. The people, following an old traditional saying in Israel (2 Samuel 20:1), said,

> What share do we have in David?
> [We have] no inheritance in the son of Jesse.
> To your tents O Israel!
> Now look to your own house, O David! (1 Kings 12:16)

Jeroboam's next paragraph was right to the point. He wrote, "The people of Israel have made me King of Israel. One of my first jobs is to rebuild Shechem, and an important part of that rebuilding is to establish our scribal school or academy. Are you willing to help me?"

After talking it over with Sharmila we decided to say that we could help. My letter to Jeroboam was quite detailed. I told him that Sharmila and I would help him, but I cautioned that at age seventy-three I could not promised a long stay.

It did not take long to pack some of our things and load them on a donkey. We learned that a caravan was leaving Tyre and going to Shechem in four days, and we decided to go to Acco for a short visit with Sharmila's parents and with our daughter, Deborah. We planned to join the caravan from Tyre at Acco and go with them to Megiddo and on to Shechem. This trip would not be too long, and we looked forward to it.

We had a good trip with the caravan. We were interested to learn that the donkeys were carrying supplies to Jeroboam for his rebuilding program in Shechem. We joked about the fact that we were in many ways a part of the freight. At least I hoped that we could rebuild the scribal community and school.

As we walked along, my thoughts turned to Ahban and how much my life had come to resemble his. He was a great teacher in the academy. Ahban means "brother of intelligence," but when he joined Absalom's rebellion, his name was changed by the administration to Ahithophel or "bother of reproach." Like Ahban, I will be seen as joining a rebellion against the House of David, even though that is not true. I had to escape; there were no other options, and there was no place for me in the House of David. Our exile, became a living example of the rebel Job's view that there is no justice.

Though doubtful, I hope that The Jerusalem Academy will collaborate with me and with the new Shechem Academy. It will not be easy, but the built-in neutrality of academies should make this possible. Also, I will ask The Hazor Academy for help, even though it has not been a productive academy for many years. Hazor once had a great academy, but it suffered a great deal of destruction about one hundred fifty years ago when great changes were happening in this country. When Egypt lost control of the many city-states it had controlled for years, there were many groups ready to destroy Hazor and take control. This would certainly include the Sea Peoples and the Philistines, or, as some of our traditions claim, perhaps Joshua and his forces. I have often wondered if the scribes at Hazor were able to rescue their library.

Our family always had an appreciation for Shechem. My mother, Keziah, and my grandfather, Gad, spent some time in Shechem before my mother and father were married. They enjoyed their experience. Then, in the early days of my father's work in the Jerusalem Academy, when he was working on *The Royal Epic*, he received help from Joshua, a minstrel from Shechem, and Elishama, who at time was a scribe from Shechem. Of course Elishama eventually came to work in Jerusalem and now is the head of The Jerusalem Academy. And then there was Samuel, who was not only from Shechem but gave his life for his friend, Jeroboam. We knew Elishama's family, and Shechem will not seem a strange place to us.

38

WHEN WE ARRIVED IN Shechem, we were welcomed by two of Jeroboam's aides. They took us to a rather nice building that Solomon had built there for his officials. Jeroboam had taken over the building, and the scribal community in Shechem had already started moving things to this center from various places in the city. The building contained a living space for Sharmila and me and an extra room for guests. There was a kitchen on the first floor. This building seemed adequate for now.

Sharmila and I unloaded our things and put them in our room, and then we went down to a larger room by the kitchen where a few scribes had just arrived with some of their things. An older man approached me and introduced himself. He said, "I am Barak, and Jeroboam put me in charge of this moving operation until you arrived."

"I am Naam, and I am pleased to meet you."

Barak answered, "Some years ago, I heard you speak at The Jerusalem Academy. I sat with my son in one of your classes; he was a student at that time."

"Where is he now?"

"He is dead. He was a close friend of Samuel, and of course you know what happened to Samuel. My son was accused of helping Samuel and Jeroboam. I understand that you were forced to leave Jerusalem, and I know that most people at The Jerusalem Academy think Solomon's soldiers killed you."

"I have heard that as well. Solomon's soldiers did kill my wife's younger sister and my sister. I am sorry to hear about your son. We have all been victims of Solomon's unjust policies. Also, I should introduce you to my wife, Sharmila. She is the daughter of a scribe from Beth-shan."

Sharmila expressed her regrets concerning Barak's son and asked, "Do you live nearby?"

"Yes. My wife and I live close to this place, and we live with our two daughter-in-laws and four grandchildren. As I said, Solomon's soldiers killed our son, who was a scribe, and our older son also died when he was working on a forced labor gang."

"I would like to meet your family," said Sharmila.

I said, "I would also like to meet them, and I would like to meet all of the scribes in Shechem who might be connected to this school either as students, interested supporters, or perhaps as teachers. Could we have such a meeting in the near future?"

"Yes. We could meet tomorrow evening in this building. I will ask everyone to bring some food, and we can have our evening meal here."

"That will be great. About how many should we expect?"

"There will be about twenty."

"I have another question. Is there any possibility of collecting manu-scripts and texts from various places in Shechem in order to build a library?"

"Yes. Many of us can bring texts from our personal collections. Also, we can copy texts that some of our minstrels keep at places like the tomb of Joseph."

"That sounds great. Elishama, who is the head of The Jerusalem Acad-emy, came from Shechem, as you probably know, and he had a friend who was a minstrel at the tomb of Joseph. His name was Joshua. Is he still here?"

"He is still here. However, he is old and does not perform anymore. You should meet him some time."

"I would like to do that."

The next morning I received a message from Jeroboam. He said that he wanted to see me, and I should come to his headquarters this morning. As I was leaving, Sharmila said, "Remember to invite Jeroboam to our din-ner and meeting with the scribes this evening."

"I'll do that. Thanks."

It was only a short walk to Jeroboam's headquarters. When I arrived, a young man ushered me into Jeroboam's office. Jeroboam was smiling and gracious. He said, "I am so glad that you said yes, and that you are now here. You have already impressed Barak, and I understand you are having a meet-ing this evening with the scribes. I will not be able to break bread with you and the others, but I will come a bit later for your meeting. As you can see I am very busy trying to get things organized, and we are starting a building project here in Shechem. So I need a few scribes to help. This evening I would like for you to assign at least two scribes, or perhaps three, to deal with some of our records, our chronicles, and to catch up on the correspondence."

"Sharmila and I are glad to be here, and we thank you for the splendid quarters. The building for the school is adequate for now, and I will appoint three scribes to fulfill your needs at once. It will take a few days to get everything organized, but I look forward to this and consider it a great opportunity. As soon as we are operating as an academy, I want to visit some other academies, and I will ask for their help. Also, we may want to go to places like Hazor and copy some of their texts for our library."

"This all sounds good. I will always be thankful for your visit with me in Egypt. That visit made our present relationship a real possibility."

With that, our meeting was over, and I left and made my way back to our quarters. I found Sharmila resting, and I joined her for a while. It was good to rest after our trip. It was all too clear that we were about to be extremely busy during the next few years. But we did not rest for long. Sharmila wanted me to help her fix something for our dinner with the scribes. Jeroboam, or someone in charge of such things, had sent us our foods supplies while I was gone, and Sharmila had arranged them in our kitchen area. We did not have much time, and since the delivery included fresh bread, I sliced some bread and cheese. Sharmila put the bread and cheese on a large plate and sat it on the table along with honey, olive oil, and olives. She also put out some wine.

Soon, Barak arrived with part of his family. Sharmila and I met his wife and one of the daughter-in-laws. The other one had stayed at home to look after the children. As others came more food was put on the table, and it was certain that we would have plenty to eat. It was a wonderful meal, and I was able to meet most of the scribes and their families. When we finished our meal, Jeroboam arrived right on time. Barak, who was in charge of the program, introduced Jeroboam to the group. Most of the scribes had known Jeroboam before he was forced to go to Egypt, and they welcomed him back as their king. Jeroboam was an attractive man, and he had a magnetic personality. People were drawn to him and to his ideas. He stood tall and spoke:

"I am glad to be with you this evening. I have known most of you even before my exile to Egypt, and it is good to see you again. I know that many of you were treated unjustly, and I hope that things will be better for all of you in the near future. This you need to know: you are essential to Israel. We cannot regain our freedom from the House of David and build a viable state without your help. For this reason, I have brought an experienced scholar, teacher and scribe to help us establish a great academy. Many of you know or have heard about Naam, who was at The Jerusalem Academy before Solomon forced him into exile. He has suffered as we have suffered, and he is ready to help us with the task before us. I intend to help Naam and you in every possible way as you begin this new phase in the life of the scribal community of Shechem. Now, I would like for Naam to tell you what he has in mind for our academy."

I stood up to speak, but I had to wait a little because everyone was talking and expressing their approval and thanks for Jeroboam's words. When things were quiet I spoke:

"You are a very fortunate group to have a leader like Jeroboam (Barak and others chanted, 'Yes! Yes! Yes-Yes-Yes!'). Not every academy has such support, and in many cases, if it has the support it does not have the freedom to do what it must do to help the state and become a great academy. So what are some of things we must do: *First*, we must preserve the past. How do we do this? We rescue and save texts and put them in our library. As teachers we should study these texts and present them to our students and learn from them. *Second*, we need to create a productive present. The state, the altar, and the academy need our skills for correspondence and for keeping records, journals, and chronicles. Also, they need psalms, poems, stories, and the wisdom of the sages. *Third*, we must provide what is necessary for a better future. This task is not easy. It involves taking some things from the past, giving them a new form in our lives and in our work, and thus putting us in a position to aim for a better future. My father, Jonathan, was a scribe, and he told me many times what Magon of Tyre said when he was interviewed for a teaching position at The Jerusalem Academy. Magon said, 'I like to teach. It is rewarding to be able to open up new worlds for students. Some of them do not take advantage of such new worlds, but a few do. Those few are the voices of the future.' My father asked, 'But why are there so few?' And Magon answered, 'Not many of us are able to be free. Our past, our families, our associates, our homeland, our religion, our health, or something has a hold on us. It is not realistic to seek complete freedom, but there has to be a certain amount of freedom in order to bring new solutions to old problems and to be a voice for the future.'

"My grandfather was also concerned about the future. Here is his poem:

It seems like it was yesterday;
When I was so young, just twenty,
And today, I am seventy!
Fifty years gone by in a day!

What happened to those days and years?
Filled with work, food, rest, sleep, and thought;
Some were dull, empty and thoughtless.
Not treasured were those days and years.

So fast the future becomes past.
It comes running, rushing to us.
Who can look to or prepare for?
My future vanished; it didn't last.

My children, they have found a way.
For most of us it's not easy;
We all crave instant approval.
The way: live the future today.

"I just want to add one point in conclusion to these remarks. We must be willing to extend our horizons. On the one hand, we love Israel and we should be proud of her traditions, but this does not mean that we should neglect the learning and wisdom of our neighbors. In order to do this we must be able to work with the languages and literature that surround us on every side. We will not be able to excel without the ability to work with Egyptian and Babylonian literature, to mention only two. Extending our horizons is another way of living for a meaningful future.

"My wife Sharmila, who is also a scribe, and I are glad to be here and thank you for your kind welcome."

39

SHARMILA AND I SPENT some time talking with the scribes and their families after the meeting, and then we helped clean up. Also, I asked Barak to help me pick out three scribes to help Jeroboam, and we also had the rest of the scribes sign up for meetings with me during the next three days. I had to get some idea of the talent and experience within our group and just how they could help. As we were getting ready for bed, Sharmila reminded me that we needed to recruit some students for our first class.

All aspects of our work proceeded smoothly with only a few problems. I was really pleased with how fast we were building our library collection. Sharmila got involved with the library project. She made lists of everything; she arranged the texts on shelves, and in many cases, she put them in jars. She soon asked for more shelves and more jars. One day she brought a text to me, saying, "This text seem old, and it is not easy to understand."

As I began to read it, I soon remembered it from many years ago at The Jerusalem Academy. When Elishama came to The Jerusalem Academy from Shechem, he brought with him many old texts and stories that my father had asked him to bring. Father needed stories from the north in order to create *The Royal Epic*. For an epic, you need stories from both the north and the south, from Israel and Judah. Such an epic is then able to unite the various factions because the people can claim the stories as their own. When my father saw this text he said that it must be one of the oldest poems in our entire collection.

We called it *The Song of Deborah and Barak* (Judges 5). It is an old song of victory and is difficult to read with many old and difficult words. I said to Sharmila, "I am so glad that you found this. It is extremely important for Jeroboam and all of us just now. Israel is not just a rebel breakaway state. This song is foundational for Israel. At one time, about two hundred years ago, this song celebrated a victory by Israel, and Israel was a new state with ten tribes. This describes Israel's beginnings before the time that Israel was related to Judah. Now we are returning to the beginnings after a short-lived attempt at unification under the House of David. Actually, father's *Royal Epic* brought together the House of David and the House of Joseph or Judah and Israel, but I must say that even though this was helpful for David's United Israel, these two states were not related in the past as *The Royal Epic* has it."

Sharmila said, "I wonder what your father would say about his work on the epic in light of our present situation?"

"I think he would say that an epic does not give one an exact picture of the past, but *The Royal Epic* did unite the country for a short time. It seemed like it was the thing to do at the time. We did not know that Solomon and his sons would ruin it. He would probably add that now each part, Judah and Israel, would need to come up with a separate epic that would unify them as a people. Such an epic can inspire and be more true to the people's past."

"Are you going to help Israel write its epic?"

"No, not me. Sharmila, we will help build an academy, but they will have to find someone to write the epic. Elishama would be the perfect one to write the epic, but he is getting old and is still the head of The Jerusalem Academy. However, starting this day, I will stress the importance of Israel's oldest song; *The Song of Deborah and Barak* could be the centerpiece for such an epic. There is another old song that they should use as well. It is *The Song of the Sea*. Some people call it *The Song of Miriam* (Exodus 15:1–18). This song celebrates the exodus from Egypt and the peoples sojourn at Mt. Sinai. If they would use Elishama's text of *The Joseph Stories*—that he worked on while still in Shechem—and then add *The Song of the Sea* plus *The Song of Deborah and Barak*, Israel would have the basic parts of its epic. I will stress this the next time I speak to the academy as a whole. As for now, I would like to ask you to make several copies of *The Song of Deborah and Barak*. I would like for the present leadership of our scribes to have copies. This will help as we try to build a foundation story for Jeroboam as he re-establishes the House of Joseph."

"I will make the copies; there will be copies ready by tomorrow evening."

"Great, and after that is finished, I think we should plan a trip to Beth-shan. I want to visit the graves of Ruth and Huraya."

"I want to do that as well. First we should write to father in Acco and find out if they could meet us in Beth-shan."

"Sharmila, your suggestion is great. Even if they cannot make the trip, they will know that we will be there."

40

THE NEXT MORNING WE got up early and enjoyed a great day. After lunch I had an appointment with Jeroboam, and we discussed some important matters. I told Jeroboam that I was pleased with the willingness of our scribes to work hard on building The Shechem Academy. Jeroboam said, "I am glad to hear this, and I heard the other day that the academy at Hazor is also trying to rebuild after major destruction during the past years. Perhaps we can help each other as both schools attempt to increase their collections of texts."

"I am certain that we can assist each other."

"Naam, I want to discuss an important matter with you. I intend to emphasize the importance of our worship of Yahweh, our God, who brought us out of Egypt. However, the people of Israel cannot continue to attend the great feasts in Jerusalem. This would only lure them back to the House of David. I think we must set up new sanctuaries in Israel. I will propose to the elders that we set up two sanctuaries at Bethel and at Dan. In these sanctuaries the symbol of God's presence will not be the Ark or the Cherubim, as in the Jerusalem temple, but rather a golden calf. We are not allowed to image our God, but we can create an animal that will serve as the foundation of his throne, though Yahweh will remain invisible. In Egypt, a God is sometimes pictured as standing on the back of an animal. Such an animal becomes the symbol of the God; the animal is not the God. What do you think about this change in our cultic centers?"

"I think it is important to do as you have suggested. Your use of the golden calves is close to the use of such animals by the Babylonians, but of course, they do picture the Gods on the backs of their animals as if in procession. It is very astute on your part to choose Bethel on our southern border and Dan in the north. All the people from north to south will have an opportunity to worship Yahweh. I hope that you will be able to find and appoint some capable priests. I found that the priests in Jerusalem were people with closed minds, and they were ignorant as well."

"I will think about your problem with priests, but I can tell you now that it will be a difficult problem to solve. I will have to appoint priests who are not sons of Levi, but this has also been done in Jerusalem."

"I have heard about that. In fact, my father told me about his conversation with the priest Abiathar on this matter. Abiathar was working with the priests of Jerusalem just as my father was working with the scribes of Jerusalem."

Finally Jeroboam said, "That is very interesting, and I will remember it. Now I must be leaving, but thanks for coming. I wanted you to know about Bethel and Dan."

I returned home and told Sharmila about the meeting. As we were talking, we heard a knock on our door. I went to the door and was greeted by a young man with a large pack. He looked tired, and I invited him in and Sharmila gave him some water. He told us that his name was Gideon and that he was a student at The Jerusalem Academy. He said, "Elishama and Khety asked me to bring an oral message to you. They were afraid to send a letter. They want to leave The Jerusalem Academy because Rehoboam and his administration have restricted their freedom. Now the state is editing all of the chronicles in order to show that Jeroboam and Israel are evil in all of their doings. To put it in a few words, Elishama, Khety, and a few of their students want to join you and help you in your new school here in Shechem."

"This is great news," I said. "How will they make this move?"

"I will return to Jerusalem and tell them of your response. Then they will begin to take their belongings—little by little—to Tamar and Khety's place near Gibeah. Their students will help them do this. Then they will send their students to Shechem over a period of about two weeks. I am from Shechem, and I will return here first with just two other students. We will set up a place for the other students at my family's house. Also, we will bring our belongings, manuscripts, and most of Elishama and Khety's things to Shechem. Finally, Elishama, Khety, and their families will make the journey."

"I am so happy to hear this," I said.

Sharmila said, "This is the best news we have had since we have been here."

I added, "Right, and we will have help, which we need, plus students. This is wonderful."

Gideon said, "In my pack, I have some of my things and the first shipment of manuscripts. I will leave the manuscripts with you, and now I must go and see my family before I return to Jerusalem. Elishama said that he would be able to stay at his family's place, but he wanted you to find a place for Khety and Tamar."

"We want to thank you for bringing us this message. Be sure to tell our friends that their help and presence will be a wonderful gift. We will await their arrival with great anticipation, and you take care."

Gideon left, and we could hardly contain our joy. Sharmila said, "Tamar and Khety can stay here in the guest room, I will clean it, and we can add items of furniture."

"That will work, and I will make sure that there is some office space they can use. Now I would like to look at these manuscripts that Elishama sent."

It did not take long for us to realize that the texts that Gideon brought belonged to mother; they were the ones that Rachel had taken to Elishama's office on the day before we left Jerusalem. What a wonderful gift! Things were really coming together.

It was difficult to wait for the arrival of our friends, but we kept busy with our preparations. About a week later, we saw Gideon again. He had returned and was staying with his family. He told us that all was going well with the plan, but everyone was being cautious because they did not want to arouse any suspicions. The others at The Jerusalem Academy still did not suspect the upcoming exodus. Another ten days passed, and Gideon stopped by again to let us know that our friends were on their way and would be here in two days. We told him to bring the other students and join us on the day they arrived. We would have dinner and celebrate.

Finally they were here. Sharmila and I were in the kitchen, when we saw Khety and Elishama approach the door. We ran and opened it before they could knock. What a happy reunion. I said, "This is one of the best days of my life. I know that this job is too much for me, and I also know that your help will make it all possible."

Elishama, who was now eighty-one, Deborah, and Rachel all looked older but healthy. Khety, who was now eighty, and Tamar also looked well. They were getting old, but they could still help. Everyone was smiling and hugging. It was a marvelous moment for all.

This all happened at about noon, so we had time for a full visit before our evening meal with the students. The conversation at times was sad, because as we remembered the good times and our hopes for the future of The Jerusalem Academy, we also asked ourselves if our work was all for nothing. I think most of us agreed that our work was valid and worth more than we could ever know. Institutions like The Jerusalem Academy flourish in their day, but they can get old and cave in to outside powers. However, they also influence many students and leave a treasure behind for future generations.

I think Elishama said it best, "I will never regret my work at The Jerusalem Academy. My family and I found friendship there and became involved in something much larger than ourselves. Our work will influence many in generations to come. And how can I ever thank Jonathan enough for introducing me to the rebel Job."

Khety said, "I agree with Elishama. I have no regrets. Also, I do not intend to ever quit working. I plan to continue my work with old friends at a new school. It will be a wonderful way to end my journey."

Tamar added, "Khety's view is mine, but I must say that at our age this move was not easy—but necessary. Our move to Shechem will give us new energy, and it is wonderful to be back in touch with friends who care."

While Tamar was speaking, Deborah was agreeing with her by voicing a "yes" several times. Then Rachel said to us, "I want to continue to help my father, but I am also glad to be with my old friends. I have always been close to both of you, and Sharmila, I hope that you and I can work on some projects together. Perhaps we could write about *The Works and Days of Female Scribes*. But first we have a lot of catching up to do."

With that Rachel and Sharmila embraced again, and then Sharmila said, "Right now we need to get ready for dinner. Soon, Gideon will be bringing the students, and I am certain they will be hungry."

Everyone helped in the kitchen and the dining area, and we were soon ready. When the students arrived, they were happy to see that their favorite teachers were safe and sound. Gideon introduced the rest of the students to Sharmila and me. They were an attractive group, and two of them were from Shechem. This will help as we try to get everyone settled and ready for their classes.

Our reunion dinner was special; it was one of the best moments of my life. And a moment it was. Our tired travelers needed to rest. As I was taking Khety and Tamar to their room, Khety said to me, "I brought the manuscripts that you left with me when you had to leave Jerusalem. I will find them among my things tomorrow."

"I will be glad to have them, and now you both need to get a good rest. I know we are going to have some great years here in Shechem. I'll see you in the morning."

Epilogue

After completing my part of our family's story, I am more aware than ever of important truths: our opinions were minority opinions; we lived with the absence of justice, but at the same time, we had a wonderful life with our friends and in our commitment to our work.

After a few years, our friends joined us in Shechem, and we were all certain that our life together in The Shechem Academy was a real blessing. We kept hearing reports about how the scribes in The Jerusalem Academy were constantly referring to "the sin of Jeroboam." He was charged with building the sanctuaries at Bethel and Dan, worshipping the golden calves, and appointing non-Levitical priests. Jeroboam did build the sanctuaries and he did appoint those priests, as had happened earlier in Jerusalem, but this does not make him a sinner. He did not worship the golden calves, but the lie that said he did was repeated in Judah until it was taken for the truth. For Jerusalem this meant that Jeroboam's kingdom would fail because sinners do not prosper.

It is apparent that Jerusalem—academy, altar, and state—is not acquainted with the rebel Job. The rebel teaches that good fortune, failure, and suffering fall on the good and the evil, even as rain falls on the good land and on the bad. One cannot expect justice from the god of the orthodox, from the state, or the god fearers, and our world does not dispense justice. Our world is beautiful, amazing, and fruitful, but its laws are firm, and the power of nature is to be respected. Jerusalem's tragedy will come upon her whenever she suffers and fails, and she too will be falsely accused: "Jerusalem is a sinner." The rebel also teaches that given our situation it is extremely important that we love each other and help the powerless.

Sharmila and I are happy here in Shechem. We do not see our children as much as we would like, and our visits to Tyre have been few. However, we did take that trip to Beth-shan, and it was helpful to tell the stories of Ruth and Huraya at their graves.

Recently, we decided to hold another community dinner to celebrate the arrival of Khety and Elishama. As Sharmila and I entered the dining room, we were welcomed by all our friends. Unknown to me, Barak had asked Jeroboam to attend. After we were finished eating, He stood and thanked us for what we had done and were doing for The Shechem Academy. Jeroboam was overjoyed that Khety and Elishama had arrived and brought some students with them. It was as if The Shechem Academy had become a reality overnight because, in a matter of a few days, Khety was teaching an Egyptian class, and Elishama was teaching a class on the story of Joseph. This activity attracted even more students, some young ones and some older scribes from our Shechem group.

Then Jeroboam thanked Rachel, Sharmila, and me, saying: "I want to give a special thanks to Rachel. Her husband, Samuel, gave his life to help me. In helping to save my life, he lost his. Rachel, I am sorry that you have had to bear this burden. Samuel was a true friend and a man of courage.

"Sharmila, I want you to know that I grieve with you for your sister, Huraya, who died in the fire at Beth-shan, and Naam, I want you to know that your sister, Ruth, is remembered here, for she also died in that fire. They did nothing to deserve such horrible treatment. These deaths and other ones, such as Barak's sons, witness the brutality engendered by Solomon's reign.

"I want to thank you all, and I want to assure you that such injustice will not be mine."

In response I said, "I can recall my exact words from the funeral service we had after the death of Huraya and Ruth. I spoke last and said: 'The great debate between father's rebel Job and the followers of the ancient Job still goes on, and it will never end. According to the ancient Job, suffering and death can be traced to one's sin and a life lived without the fear of God. But the rebel Job voices a hearty *no* to such nonsense. During natural events, such as floods, suffering falls on the innocent and the guilty with equal intensity. But when we see the suffering caused by people, it appears that the innocent suffer more than the guilty. They suffer more because in most cases, the guilty are usually identified with the powerful. This is one reason there is no justice, and it is the reason the rebel Job stands up for the cause of the powerless. Our loved ones lost their lives; they were innocent and powerless and could not stand against Solomon's troops. I have to take some blame for involving these fine young people in the fight against

Solomon's policies. I did have some indication that my family and friends were of the same mind, but still, to lose a young member of your family is a tragic blow. I can only hope that when we relate this story to others, they will understand that those in power have slaughtered the innocent.'"

"Now Jeroboam, we thank you for remembering our loved ones and for your understanding. Also we want to thank you for allowing us to live and to work as free scribes in this free community. Here, we can live the future now."

Afterword

THE FOLLOWING NOTES AND comments allow me to expand items that were briefly mentioned and hopefully will alow the reader to pursue the subjects that are discussed in this book.

Acknowledgments: My teachers were Quirinus Breen (History, University of Oregon), Toyozo W. Nakarai (Semitic Languages and Literature, Butler University), and Cyrus H. Gordon (Mediterranean Studies, Brandeis University).

Colleagues who have been helpful: Hans Dieter Betz, John B. Cobb Jr., Robert W. Funk, Burton L. Mack, and Eugene H. Peters.

Students who have assisted me with projects are: Kevin Clark, K. C. Hanson, Donn F. Morgan, F. Brent Knutson, Stan Rummel, and Duane E. Smith.

In my "Acknowledgments" I note that *Living without Justice* is the final book of *The Jerusalem Trilogy*. In these historical novels, I have set the narrative in the time of the Davidic Monarchy. Talking about scribes in Jerusalem in the tenth century BCE during the Davidic Monarchy is not a popular point of view today in university centers. The tendency is to characterize the Davidic Monarchy as pure fiction from a much later period. I do not agree with this characterization for many reasons. To me, David was a real person who ruled Israel in the tenth century BCE. In folk tradition of any kind, the lives of heroes are typically embellished, and it is difficult to invent the protagonist. A later novelist did not invent George Washington, but there is no doubt that the story about a cherry tree can be classified as an embellishment. David's battle with Goliath is also an embellishment, as I have noted in these novels. Moreover, in Hebrew traditions, it is not clear who killed Goliath. Nevertheless, both George and David were real persons.

Those who deny the reality of the Davidic Monarchy often speak of Jerusalem as a village. They do this despite the existence of the Amarna letters from the ruler of Jerusalem to the King of Egypt. In the "Preface to the Second Edition" of my book, *Genesis, A Royal Epic*, 2nd ed. (Eugene, OR: Cascade Books, 2011) xi–xii, I note that I am more convinced than ever of my position: "One reason for my optimism is the discovery in Jerusalem— or to be more specific, in the City of David, the oldest part of Jerusalem—of a cuneiform tablet. There is a good article on this. See Eilat Mazar, Wayne Horowitz, Takayoshi Oshima, and Yuval Goren, "A Cuneiform Tablet from the Ophel in Jerusalem," *Israel Exploration Journal* 60 (2010) 4–21. Actually the tablet is just a fragment (designated Jerusalem 1), and that means we cannot say much about the content. However, by analyzing the signs carefully, the authors, who studied it, have determined that the scribe, who wrote this tablet, had a better hand than the two scribes who wrote tablets 285–291 of the Amarna letters. The ruler of Jerusalem, Abdi-Heba, sent these letters to the Egyptian Pharaoh (see William L. Moran, editor and translator, *The Amarna Letters* [Baltimore: Johns Hopkins University Press, 1987]). So the authors say:

> In fact, it is our impression that the scribe of Jerusalem 1 shows greater expertise than the scribes of Abdi-Heba in EA 285–290. Our conclusion, then, is that the scribe of the Jerusalem fragment seems capable of producing high-quality international-standard scribal work, a conclusion that is also supported by the shape of the fragment, as indicated by the surviving piece of the left edge, which seems to us to be closer to the Mesopotamian ideal than most tablets from the cuneiform west.

This new information may not prove my view that there was a scribal school in Jerusalem before and during the Davidic monarchy, but it certainly points to a great teacher and at least two other scribes. My view is based on the fact that great centers needed and had scribal schools. In my novels, Magon of Tyre was such a scribe and a great teacher of Babylonian cuneiform literature."

Now I would like to add some important material that my editor, K. C. Hanson, suggested to me. This material consists of Nadav Na'aman's two essays concerning scribal activity in Jerusalem. They are: "Sources and Composition in the History of David" and "Sources and Composition in the History of Solomon." These essays can be found in Na'aman's *Ancient*

Israel's History and Historiography: The First Temple Period, Collected Essays 3 (Winona Lake, IN: Eisenbrauns, 2006) 79–101 and 23–37.

As a result of Na'aman's studies he concludes, "I would like to suggest epigraphic evidence that supports the assumption that scribal activity had already taken place in Jerusalem by the tenth century BCE."

The use of hieratic numerals (i.e., Egyptian cursive numerals) by the scribes of Israel and Judah has been noted in the ostraca from Lachish. Na'aman says, "It is clear that the hieratic signs entered the Hebrew script before the ninth century BCE. Writing in hieratic is known from southern Canaan in the late thirteenth–twelfth centuries BCE." Also Na'aman (following Goldwasser), suggests that Egyptian-trained scribes taught local scribes, "who passed on their knowledge to the new court of Israel, probably in the Age of the United Monarchy." Later, the Egyptians did not use the hieratic numerals. "We may conclude that the appearance of hieratic numerals and signs in the Hebrew script of Israel and Judah supports the assumption that scribal activity was introduced in the court of Jerusalem no later than the time of Solomon and possibly by David's time."

If the Egyptians taught Hebrew scribes to use hieratic numerals, I would suggest that the Egyptians taught them how to tell stories. See "The Story of Sinuhe," in Fisher, *Tales from Ancient Egypt* (Eugene, OR: Cascade Books, 2010) 5–29. On 17 n. 47 of that volume, I discuss the "battle of champions." The story of David's battle with Goliath follows the basic form of the story of Sinuhe's battle with the hero of Retenu.

One of the most interesting essays on scribal activity and the production of Genesis at the time of the Davidic Monarchy is that of Benjamin Mazar's "The Historical Background of the Book of Genesis," *Journal of Near Eastern Studies* 28 (1969) 73–83. I have noted this in the "Introduction" to my *Genesis, A Royal Epic*, 2nd ed., 7 n. 13. Here I quote Mazar from p. 74 of his essay where he states, "It is within reason that Genesis was given its original written form during the time when the Davidic empire was being established, and that additional supplements of later authors were only intended to help bridge the time gap for contemporary readers, and had no decisive effect on its contents or overall character."

Chapter Two: The discussion about Job can be seen in greater detail in my four books: *Who Hears the Cries of the Innocent?* (Willits, CA: Fisher Publications, 2003), *The Minority Report*, 2nd ed. (Eugene, OR: Cascade Books, 2013), *The Rebel Job* (Willits, CA: Fisher Publications, 2006), and *The Many Voices of Job* (Eugene, OR: Cascade Books, 2009).

Chapter Eight: Sharmila's name means "alabaster" in Ugaritic. I learned it is also a modern name with some other meanings from Sharmila Sen, a general editor for the Humanities at Harvard University Press.

Chapter Nine: I have translated *The Enchanted Prince* into English. It is obvious that Naam's translation into Hebrew does not exist except in this novel. Written later than *The Story of the Shipwrecked Sailor* (1800 BCE), it is a story from the New Kingdom in about 1400 BCE. The translation of this story has been more difficult for all translators than the translation of *The Story of the Shipwrecked Sailor*, and the end of this story is missing. I have written an ending, much like the endings in *The Story of the Shipwrecked Sailor* and *The Story of Sinuhe*, in which the hero returns to Egypt for his proper burial. The ending is a happy ending, and therefore, I do not call this story *The Story of the Doomed Prince* as others have done in the past. Also, I do not use the descriptive title, *The Prince and His Three Fates*. Instead, I have called it *The Enchanted Prince*. In late Egyptian literature if you mention an Egyptian king, queen, or any honored person, you immediately say, "May he/she *live*, be *prosperous*, be *healthy*." In this translation, this phrase is abbreviated to "l.p.h." (The Egyptian scribes gave the first hieroglyph for the first and third of these three words and the second hieroglyph for the second word.)

The Enchanted Prince is about a young prince who traveled to Naharin. Naharin, in Egyptian literature, refers to the Mitanni Kingdom of northern Mesopotamia (in the area of modern-day Kirkuk or ancient Arrapha, and to the west). Khor is also mentioned and is a term for Syria. The travels of this young prince remind us of the journey of Sinuhe in *The Story of Sinuhe* (1900 BCE).

The theme of our story will probably be known to most readers, and certainly to those who have read other tales about contests to see who could win the king's daughter. The tale of Rapunzel has the girl, the tower, the window, and the prince, but the other details are different.

The text used for this translation can be found in Alan H. Gardiner, *Late Egyptian Stories*, Bibliotheca Aegyptica I (Brussels: Edition de la Fondation Egyptologique Reine Elisabeth, 1932; reprinted, 1981) 1–9. Gardiner's suggestions for text restorations were usually followed. I have been assisted by referring to the translation of Edward F. Wente Jr. in *The Literature of Ancient Egypt*, edited by William Kelly Simpson (New Haven: Yale University Press, 1973). Also, I have benefited from Miriam Lichtheim's *Ancient Egyptian Literature*, vol. 2 (Berkeley: University of California Press, 1976). In addition, I have received help from many translated examples in Sir Alan Gardiner's

Egyptian Grammar, 2nd ed. (London: Oxford University Press, 1950). With great appreciation, I have used Adolf Erman and Hermann Grapow's *Wörter-buch der ägyptischen Sprache* (Berlin: Akademie-Verlag, 1955).

According to John A. Wilson (*The Culture of Ancient Egypt* [Chicago: University of Chicago Press, 1951]), Thut-mose III (1490–1436 BCE) had troubles with the Mitanni (or Naharin) Kingdom, but Thut-mose IV (1406–1398 BCE) married a Mitanni princess. Amen-hotep III (1398–1361 BCE) married two princesses from Mitanni, but perhaps Tadu-Kepa, daughter of Tushratta, came into the harem of Akh-en-Aton (1369–1353 BCE). Therefore, this story would not sound strange to an Egyptian's ear. I have published this story and four others in Fisher, *Tales from Ancient Egypt: The Birth of Stories*.

Chapter Twelve and Thirteen: The translation of Sinuhe is mine. Naam's translation into Hebrew does not exist, but I believe that Hebrew scribes did translate many things. I have only given some parts of the translation. As noted above, I have published *Tales from Ancient Egypt*, which contains *The Story of Sinuhe, The Enchanted Prince, The Shipwrecked Sailor, Wen-Amon,* and *A Dialogue between a Man and His Ba*.

Miriam Lichtheim says that *The Story of Sinuhe* "is the crown jewel of Middle Kingdom literature" (*Ancient Egyptian Literature*, vol. 1, 11). According to Lichtheim, the tomb is the setting for such a jewel; it is at the tomb that autobiography was born and true narrative literature took its shape. This is important in terms of Egyptian literature, and it is a most important event for world literature. *The Story of Sinuhe* is from about 1960 BCE in the Twelfth Dynasty. This jewel followed the style of the older autobiographies of Weni and Harkhuf from the Sixth Dynasty (2300–2150 BCE), but *Sinuhe* surpassed all earlier examples. Lichtheim's comment on *Sinuhe* reads: "Through its beginning and its ending, the story is given the form of the tomb-autobiography in which the narrator looks back on his completed life" (235 n. 26).

Besides Lichtheim, other translators have been helpful in my work including John Wilson in *Ancient Near Eastern Texts*, 3rd ed., edited by James B. Pritchard (Princeton: Princeton University Press, 1969), and William Kelly Simpson in *The Literature of Ancient Egypt*, edited by William Kelly Simpson (New Haven: Yale University Press, 1973). In addition, I have received help from many translated examples in Sir Alan Gardiner's *Egyptian Grammar*.

In Chapter Thirteen I mention another tradition about the killing of Goliath. This can be found in 2 Samuel 21:19, where Elhanan is mentioned as the one who killed Goliath. But in 1 Chronicles 20:5 this information is changed. Here Elhanan kills the brother of Goliath. Later scribes harmonized these conflicting traditions with such changes.

Chapter Fourteen: In this chapter I refer to Nathan and Hushai and their editing of *Job II*. This story is from my book *The Minority Report*.

Chapter Fifteen: About one thousand years after *The Story of Sinuhe*, *The Journey of Wen-Amon* was written. During the last part of the reign of Ramses XI (about 1090–1080 BCE), the rule of Egypt was divided between Heri-Hor of Thebes (in the south) and Ne-su-Ba-neb-Ded (Smendes) of Tanis (in the north). Wen-Amon was from Thebes and he was sent to Byblos in Phoenicia to buy cedar for the divine barque of Amon-Re.[1] I take the position along with many others that this story, or report, is about a real journey. In any case, it tells us a great deal about Egypt and Phoenicia at this time. One section of the story is badly damaged, and the ending is missing as well. But the report is usually taken as proof that Wen-Amon did return to Egypt and wrote this account of his travels.

The text I use is from Gardiner's *Late-Egyptian Stories*, 62–76. As I have said in the notes above, I have been helped many times by the translations of John Wilson, Miriam Lichtheim, and Edward F. Wente Jr. I have learned from them, and I depart from their work only when the evidence forces my hand. They have made some mistakes, and I am certain that I have made my share. But our work is a real adventure, and it is a lot of fun to be able to get close to the author of this report. We cannot get inside his head, but we can get close to him.

Chapter Seventeen: In this chapter, I deal with Solomon's rise to power. Adonijah tried to become king and was backed by Joab and Abiathar. I suggested that all three of them *plotted* a rebellion against David. The Hebrew text of 1 Kings 1:7 reads, "His words (Hebrew *dabar*, "speech/talk") were with Joab . . . and with Abiathar." Most translations use a neutral word "conferred," but in fact they were "plotting." We have the same situation in 2 Samuel 3:17 where Abner is doing more than just "conferring" with the

---

1. This information is available in many places, e.g., Wilson, *The Culture of Ancient Egypt*, 289–92. Also in Lichtheim, *Ancient Egyptian Literature*, vol. 2, 224; and Wente in *The Literature of Ancient Egypt*, 142.

Elders of Israel. This use of "talking with" in the sense of plotting is also present in an Akkadian text from Ugarit. See *The Claremont Ras Shamra Tablets*, edited by Loren R. Fisher (Rome: Pontifical Biblical Institute, 1971) 11–12. Here the king of Amurru is not allowed to "talk with" (*i-dáb-bu-ub*) or "plot with" his exiled sister.

Chapter Eighteen: If it really happened, Solomon's marriage to Pharaoh's daughter gives any author a lot to imagine. But there are some factual matters to consider. For this material it is best to start with Sir Alan Gardiner's *Egypt of the Pharaohs* (Oxford: Clarendon, 1964). Pages 316–29 in Chapter XII of Gardiner give us a lot of details concerning the Twenty-first Dynasty. Though "chronological uncertainties" make Gardiner cautious about which Pharaoh gave his daughter to Solomon, the information he collects makes it seem probable that the Pharaoh was Psusennes II. (Also see Gordon, Cyrus H., and Gary A. Rendsburg. *The Bible and the Ancient Near East*. 4th ed. New York: Norton, 1997. 208, for this conclusion). Others see the Pharaoh as Siamun, who captured Gezer: see John Bright, *A History of Israel*, 2nd ed. (Philadelphia: Westminster, 1972) 207–8; Yohannan Aharoni, *The Land of the Bible*, trans. A. F. Rainey (Philadelphia: Westminster, 1967) 275; William W. Hallo and William Kelly Simpson, *The Ancient Near East*, 2nd ed. (New York: Harcourt Brace Jovanovich, 1998) 284. The best treatment of these matters (and the one I have used in this story) is by Pierre Montet, who excavated at Tanis, and I take it from his book *Egypt and the Bible*, trans. Leslie R. Keylock (Philadelphia: Fortress, 1968) 35–40. Also Étienne Drioton and Jacques Vandier follow much of Montet's work in their *L'Égypte*, Les Peuples de l'Orient Méditerranéen 2 (Paris: Presses Universitaires de France, 1952) 517–25. It is not an easy call, but I follow the French.

Chapter Nineteen: For a detailed essay on the material in this chapter, see Loren R. Fisher, "From Ugarit to Gades: Mediterranean Veterinary Medicine," *Maarav* 5–6 (1990) 207–20. The discussion of Solomon's wisdom in 1 Kings was greatly expanded in later times. After all, Naam was only handed a few lines about Solomon's abilities, but the following lines show the expansion:

> Elohim gave Solomon wisdom, tremendous understanding, and an expansive mind like the sand that is on the seashore. The wisdom of Solomon was greater than that of the Bene-Qedem and from all the wisdom of Egypt. He was wiser than any human: than Ethan the Ezrahite, Heman, Calcol, and Darda, Bene-Mahol; his

name became known among the surrounding states. He produced three thousand proverbs; his songs were a thousand and five. He spoke concerning the trees, from the cedar that is in Lebanon to the hyssop that comes out from the wall. He spoke about the domesticated animals, about the birds, about the reptiles, and about the fish. They came from all the peoples to hear the wisdom of Solomon [and] from all the kings of the earth who had heard his wisdom. (1 Kings 5:9–14; English 4:29–34)

Chapter Twenty: See John Gray, *I & II Kings*, Old Testament Library (Philadelphia: Westminster, 1963), for a decent handling of these materials relating to Solomon's reign. See p. 231 for comments on Solomon's building program and on his store-cities. However, we remain critical of some of this work. Solomon's store-cities may be equated with the store-cities of Exodus 1:11, but these are not the store-cities built by Joseph. In fact, the translation of the Hebrew *'are hamiskenot* ("behind store-cities") is difficult. Gray's translation of 1 Kings 10:28–29 is strange: "Now the source of Solomon's horses was Musri and Kue; the king's dealers got them from Kue, and a chariot came up by export from Musri at one hundred shekels of silver and a horse at fifty, and so also the kings of the Hittites and the kings of the Aramaeans got them by export through them." The Jewish Publication Society's *Tanakh* follows the Hebrew text with six hundred for a chariot and one hundred fifty for a horse. Also they keep the Hebrew *Mizraim* and note that this word meaning "Egypt" might refer to Musri, which was near Kue in southeast Asia Minor. These verses are difficult, but I think the general sense is clear. Certainly Kue was a good source for the horses, and the chariots "came up" (or north) from Egypt; they did not come down from Musri. Egypt made chariots from imported wood and also they received many chariots and horses from northern states in the form of tribute. Again see Drioton and Vandier, *L'Égypte*, 467. The Egyptians received "chevaux et chars" from these states. Apparently Solomon's "dealers" made these purchases for him and also sold some to other northern kings.

For the agreement between Solomon and Hiram note 1 Kings 5:21–25; 9:10–14; and 9:26–28. Their shipping business is dealt with in 1 Kings 9:26–28; 10:11–12; and 10:22.

First Kings 9:4–9 is an example of the conditional covenant. First Kings 11 is a later admission that Solomon's reign was finished.

Chapter Twenty-One: I am very interested in what is said concerning Jeroboam in 1 Kings 11:26. The text reads: *wayyarrem yad bamelek*, "He raised [his] hand against the King." This means that Jeroboam rebelled against Solomon. It is interesting that when the same idiom is used in 2 Samuel 18:28 and 20:21 everything is the same except the verb in 2 Samuel is *nasa'* and the possessive suffix is supplied in each case. For an Akkadian-Hurrian bilingual text from Ugarit that uses this idiom, see J. Nougayrol and E. Laroche, "Le Bilingue Accado-Hourrite," in *Le Palais Royal D'Ugarit III* (Paris: Imprimerie Nationale, 1955) 309–24. This text is also discussed by E. A. Speiser in "Akkadian Documents from Ras Shamra," *Journal of the American Oriental Society* 75 (1955) 154–65. For an English translation, see W. G. Lambert, *Babylonian Wisdom Literature* (Oxford: Clarendon, 1960) 116. Lambert's translation, however, is difficult for me to accept.

Chapter Twenty-Two: Jonathan's funeral is patterned after the other funerals in my novels. Gad's funeral occurs in *The Jerusalem Academy* (462–65), and the funeral for the scroll of *The Rebel Job* is in *The Minority Report* (181–93).

Chapter Twenty-Three: Elhanan is credited with killing Goliath (2 Samuel 21:19), and later scribes, who wanted to harmonize the traditions, changed things in 1 Chronicles 20:5, where they say that Elhanan killed the brother of Goliath. I have given this information above in my note for Chapter Thirteen, but in this chapter, I am suggesting that this idea that Elhanan killed Goliath's brother was one way of dealing with the two traditions long before the Chronicler's account.

In 1 Kings 9:20–22, there is a similar claim that Solomon did not make slaves of Israel, but in 1 Kings 11:26–40, Jeroboam is put in charge of the forced labor of the north. One could say that forced labor does not equal slavery, but that would be just playing with words. It is interesting that in 2 Chronicles 8:9 the denial tradition is maintained and the Jeroboam tradition is left out.

Chapter Twenty-Four: See my *Tales from Ancient Egypt*, 62, for the quote from *Wen-Amon* in context. Also see note 28: This is like the Hebrew title for Chronicles of kings: *sefer divrey hayyamim*, "the scroll of the words/ acts of the days." See 1 Kings 14:29. Aage Bentzen says, "The kings of pre-Israelite Canaan had their *books* in which the *acts of their ancestors* were written. This is a very important fact to be taken into account in the present discussion of the significance of oral tradition." He goes on to refer to this passage in Wen-Amon. See Bentzen, *Introduction to the Old Testament*, vol. 1 (Copenhagen: Gad, 1952) 245.

Chapter Thirty: *"Partir—c'est mourir un peu"* (Parting—it is dying a little). John Bayley calls attention to this French saying in his "Introduction" to Boris Pasternak's *Doctor Zhivago* (New York: Pantheon, 1991) xx. I could not stop thinking about these words that so aptly describe the central and tragic theme in *Doctor Zhivago*. In part, it was because I had dealt with this idea in a couple of poems in April of 2005 and in February of 2006, and the phrase was important to my understanding of "process thought" and my interest in "ancient autobiography/biography" composed for the tomb. But this enchanting phrase was also related to my love of *Out of Africa* and *Doctor Zhivago*. All of this helped me in writing the poem "Death Is a Final Parting." For this poem I am also indebted in part to Charles Hartshorne. See his *Omnipotence and Other Theological Mistakes* (Albany: SUNY Press, 1984) 36 and 104–10.

See my *Genesis, A Royal Epic*, 28–30 and 35, for more details on the treatment of the dead and the burial of Aqhat. I have discussed the burial of Saul in great detail in *The Jerusalem Academy*, 249–54. For the quotation from Job 19:25, see my *The Many Voices of Job*, 65, and also my *Tales from Ancient Egypt*, 77 n. 22.

Chapter Thirty-one: I should say that we do not know enough about ancient Tyre, but we do know a lot about Phoenician shipping because of the work of Bob Ballard. See Rick Gore's article "Ancient Ashkelon," *National Geographic* 199.1 (2001) 64–93. On pages 91–93 there is a brief report on Bob Ballard's discovery of two Phoenician shipwrecks off the coast of Ashkelon. These ships were loaded with cargo. One of them had at least four-hundred five-gallon jars of wine. Another good source for shipping is George F. Bass, "Sea and River Craft in the Ancient Near East," in *Civilizations of the Ancient Near East*, edited by Jack M. Sasson, vol. 3 (New York: Scribner, 1995) 1421–31.

Chapter Thirty-Two: For the Tell el-Amarna Tablets, see Moran, ed. and trans., *The Amarna Tablets*. For the Pharaoh's letter to Aziru see text 162 in Moran's book. In this text, Gubla is the same as Gebal and much later the Greeks called it Byblos. My translations are slightly different from Moran's. Part of the reason for this stems from the fact I have written an essay on double attribution in the writings of Egyptian scribes. The essay:

"Double Attribution in a Letter from Egypt to Ugarit (RS 88.2158)," *JAOS* 130 (2010) 619–21. Naam has been translating some Egyptian stories so he is aware of this habit of Egyptian scribes, and it shows even when they write Babylonian, and especially when they translate from Egyptian to Babylonian. I make this observation from my recent work on *The Journey of Wen-Amon* (see Fisher, *Tales from Ancient Egypt*). The dialogue in Wen-Amon has both single and double attribution. The following passages show the double attribution:

1. *"And he said to me,* 'Now see here, seeing that documents (and) letters are not in your hand, where is the cedar ship that Ne-su-Ba-neb-Ded gave to you? Where is (1, 55) its Syrian crew? Did he not give you to the captain of a foreign ship in order to kill you and throw you to the sea? With whom would they seek the God? Not with me.' *Thus he said to me."* (1, 53—1, 57)

2. *"And I said to him,* 'I am making (this) trip to bring back the timber for the great and noble barque of Amon-Re, King of the Gods. What your father did, what (2, 5) your grandfather did, you will do it as it was done.' *I said to him."* (2, 4—2, 5)

3. *"And I said to him,* 'It is not true. These are not silly trips, which I am on. There is no ship on the River that does not belong to Amon. The sea is his, and the Lebanon is his of which you say, "It is mine." . . . I shall send him to them saying, "Have it brought until I have come (again) to the south, and I shall have all, yes all, of the debt that has not been paid brought to you."' *Thus I said to him."* (2, 22—2, 37)

Chapter Thirty-Three: The ten tablets dealing with Tyre's past are tablets 146–155 and found in Moran's *The Amarna Letters*, 232–42. However, when Naam discusses these, he numbers them 1–10. In other words, number 1 = 146. Moran's translations are useful, but they are not always complete or accurate. In 147, 148, 149, and 152, he translates, "my Gods" in the singular, "my God." But in 151 he seems to be forced to use the plural because there is also the singular: "To the king, my Sun, my God, my Gods." Albright in *Ancient Near Eastern Texts*, 484, translates the plural form as "my pantheon." The plural probably refers to two gods, Akh-en-Aton and Aton. I suggest this because of a quotation by John A. Wilson in *The Culture of Ancient Egypt*, 223. Wilson says, "The most important observation about Amarna religion is that there were two gods central to the faith, and not one. Akh-en-Aton and his family worshipped the Aton, and everybody else worshipped Akh-en-Aton *as a god.*" In the next chapter I credit Zadok with this observation.

In *The Jerusalem Academy,* the first edition, I refer to the language of Tyre as Phoenician (pp. 200 and 273), as the Greeks called it, and also the name we usually use for this early period. It is a convenient name but anachronistic. In this book, I use "the language of Tyre" to refer to the old language of Tyre. This usage is the same as in the Hebrew Bible. There the language of the Hebrews is not called Hebrew but "the language of Canaan" in Isaiah 19:18 and the "language of Judah" in 2 Kings 18:26–28.

Chapter Thirty-Four: See W. F. Albright, "The Egyptian Correspondence of Abimilki, Prince of Tyre," *Journal of Egyptian Archaeology* 23 (1937) 180–203.

Chapter Thirty-Five: The Egyptian *Niwet-'Amon,* "The city of Amon," is written and pronounced *No' 'Amon* in Hebrew (see Nahum 3:8). An even older name for Thebes in Egyptian is *Waset.* When Khety and Naam visit the entire complex at Waset, they are interested in the work and military campaigns of Thut-mose III, Amen-hotep III, and Seti I. The lists of the cities they conquered can be found in J. Simons, *Handbook for the Study of Egyptian Topographical Lists Relating to Western Asia* (Leiden: Brill, 1937).

Chapter Thirty-Six: In 1964 my son, Dan Fisher, and I spent some time at ancient Ugarit. In many ways Naam's trip is a re-enactment of our 1964 trip. In our case a young friend from Beirut took us north to his home in Latakia or ancient Ramitha. His mother told me how she preserved her olives. Later, I was surprised to discover similar methods in the Roman authors, Varro and Columella, from about two thousand years earlier.

For an introduction to the city of ancient Ugarit, see Marguerite Yon, *The City of Ugarit at Tell Ras Shamra* (Winona Lake, IN: Eisenbrauns, 2006); and for a detailed study about anchors from Ugarit and other port cities see Honor Frost, "Anchors Sacred and Profane," in *Ras Shamra-Ougarit VI, Arts et Industries de la Pierre,* edited by Marguerite Yon (Paris: Éditions Recherche sur les Civilisations, 1991) 355–410.

In *Ras Shamra-Ougarit VII* (p. 31) there is an unbroken text (RS 34.138) from the king of Carchemish like the broken one found by Naam.

Chapter Thirty-Seven: I translate 1 Kings 12:20. The similar saying in 2 Samuel 20:1 is different. It does not start with a question, and it does not have a fourth line. "We have no share in David. / And we have no inheritance in the son of Jesse. / Every man to his tent, O Israel." For the material on Ahban see *The Jerusalem Academy*, Chapter XLIII.

Chapter Thirty-Eight: Hazor (Hatsura EA 148:41–42, from Tyre; from Hazor 227:3; 228:4, 15, 23; and 364:18). On Hazor, see Joshua 11:1–15.

Chapter Thirty-Nine: My discussion of "The Song of the Sea/Miriam" and "The Song of Deborah and Barak" depend on the work David Noel Freedman, "Early Israelite History in the Light of Early Israelite Poetry," in *Unity and Diversity: Essays in the History, Literature, and Religion of the Ancient Near East*, ed. H. Goedicke and J. J. M. Roberts (Baltimore: Johns Hopkins University Press, 1975). Freedman also depends on the work of many others, including Marvin L. Chaney, who wrote his Harvard dissertation on *The Song of Deborah* (1976). He also wrote a summary for a Society of Biblical Literature meeting, which has been helpful ("The Song of Deborah and the Peasants' War").

Chapter Forty: For a discussion about Jeroboam and the golden calves, see Roland de Vaux, OP, *Ancient Israel: Its Life and Institutions*, trans. John McHugh (London: Darton, Longman & Todd, 1961) 332–36.

Other recent books by Loren R. Fisher

Genesis, A Royal Epic, 2nd ed.
Introduction, Translation, and Notes

The Jerusalem Academy, 2nd ed.
A Story of the Production of *Genesis, A Royal Epic*

The Minority Report: Silenced by Religion, 2nd ed.
A Story of the Creation of *The Rebel Job*

The Story of the Shipwrecked Sailor
Translated from the Egyptian by Loren R. Fisher ·
Illustrated by John Fisher

The Rebel Job: Revised Edition
Translation and Commentary

The Many Voices of Job
Translation and Structure of the Entire Book

Tales from Ancient Egypt:
The Birth of Stories

The Eloquent Peasant